Love

Loss

Revenge

By

Graysen Morgen

2012

Love Loss Revenge © 2012 Graysen Morgen

Triplicity Publishing, LLC

ISBN-10: 0988619601

ISBN-13: 978-0-9886196-0-9

All rights reserved. No part of this publication may be reproduced, distributed, or transmitted in any form without permission.

This is a work of fiction. Names, characters, places, and incidents are the product of the author's imagination and are used fictitiously. Any resemblance to actual persons, living or dead, business establishments, events, or locales is entirely coincidental.

Printed in the United States of America

First Edition – 2012

Cover Design: Triplicity Publishing, LLC

Interior Design: Triplicity Publishing, LLC

Also by Graysen Morgen

Falling Snow

Fate vs. Destiny

Just Me

Natural instinct

Secluded Heart

Submerged

Acknowledgements

Special thanks to Lee Fitzsimmons, the person who spends countless hours correcting my mistakes. I promise to get rid of the brain worms eventually.

Dedication

This book is graciously dedicated to my grandmother. Without her, books would probably not be a big part of my life. Nanna, I finally figured out who did it.

Chapter One

Rian Casey finished brushing her teeth and spit the last of the toothpaste remnants into the sink. She towel dried her short, dark hair and stepped out of the bathroom. The platinum gray bedding comforter was in a wad on the floor at the foot of the bed and the white rumpled sheets were tangled around the slender nude body in her bed. Her long, wavy, blond hair fanned across the pillow behind her head. Most of her back and a partial thigh was exposed revealing tan skin that contrasted nicely against the white sheets. Rian smiled and silently thanked whoever it was with the powers above that brought this amazing woman into her life two years ago.

When Rian was finished dressing in a black pants suit with a white blouse underneath, she walked out of the closet quietly. The beautiful woman in her bed was grinning up at her as she pulled the sheet back and patted the bed. Rian walked over and sat down next to her.

"Good morning," Rian said as she sat down.

"It would be a lot better if you got back in here with me." Her voice was so sweet and innocent it played Rian's heartstrings like a finely tuned guitar every time she spoke. Rian brushed a strand of hair from her cheek revealing a beautiful face with a small slightly pointed nose, high cheekbones, and perfect, kissable lips that were thin with just enough fullness. She was still taken aback every time she looked at the eyes staring back at her. The alluring woman smiling up at Rian had a condition called Heterochromia causing one of her eyes to be bright green while the other was as blue as the ocean.

"Ari," Rian sighed and grazed her fingers over her soft cheek. There was nothing more that she would rather do, but as a Senior Special Agent with the FBI she didn't get leisure time.

"I'm only teasing you. I know you have big bad criminals to go after today. I just hate spending our anniversary apart," Ari said as she slipped her hand between the buttons on Rian's shirt and stroked the firm muscles of her stomach.

Rian closed her eyes and allowed the caress. Ari Turner knew the right buttons to push, but what she didn't know was there were no buttons. The usually cool, calm, and collected government agent completely crumbled the very first time she saw Ari and was head over heels in love with her ever since. Most of the time, it wasn't even a touch that provoked their lovemaking. Instead, it was a simple smile or casual eye contact that sent Rian's libido into high gear and her blood flowing south. Rian eased her hand away and stood up.

Ari tossed the sheet to the side and slid out of the bed. Rian's mouth watered as she watched the nude body moving towards her. Ari's long hair fell in loose waves against her chest, grazing her perky round breasts with tiny pink nipples peeking out between the strands. At only five foot three she was petite with the right amount of delicate curves and toned muscles from hours of cardio and yoga. Rian watch the muscles move in her tan legs starting at her ankles, sliding up her calves, and across her thighs to the runway strip of hair at the base of her legs that was the same light shade as the hair on her head and so thin it almost wasn't there. Her torso and flat stomach formed a subtle hourglass shape with a tiny diamond studded bar piercing the top of her navel.

Ari ran her hand through her hair and tossed it over her shoulder as she slowly walked across the room. She knew she would win this little game of cat and mouse, she always did. She couldn't help starting something she knew Rian would be willing to finish. She craved Rian like the Earth craved the Sun. Almost like she needed her to survive. She stepped so close she could feel the silk from Rian's suit brushing her skin. She ran her hands up Rian's chest inside her jacket and pushed it off her shoulders until it fell silently to the floor. Then, she ran her fingers through Rian's hair and pulled the taller woman down to meet her waiting lips in a searing kiss that started agonizingly slow.

Rian ran her tongue across the outside of Ari's bottom lip before taking what was being offered. She kissed her with every ounce of her soul, becoming so lost she was gasping for air, but reluctant to break the contact. She shivered from the hunger she knew only this woman could quell. The blood rushed from her head and throbbed in her crotch. She'd heard of being deeply in love, but she was bordering on addiction where Ari was concerned and she loved every minute of it.

When Ari moved one of her hands from Rian's hair to her chest and pinched her nipple through her blouse and bra Rian wrapped her hands around Ari's ass at the base of her thighs and easily lifted her. Ari wrapped her legs around Rian's waist and pulled back enough to look into her smoky gray eyes.

"I'm so wet baby, you're going to get it on your pants," she said.

Rian grinned and went in for another breathless kiss and rocked Ari's crotch against her at the same time. She broke away from the kiss and ran her lips and tongue tenderly down the soft skin of her neck and across her collarbone. She turned her head to the side and looked at the different colored eyes watching her.

"Do you really think I'm worried about a pair of pants?" She asked as she bit down on the soft skin of her shoulder and snaked her tongue out and ran it over the sensitive spot. She smiled when she felt Ari's hips move against her involuntarily. She knew Ari was wet, she felt it on the tips of her fingers when she picked her up. Ari answered her with another arousing kiss as she opened the buttons of her blouse one at a time.

Rian kicked her shoes off and walk towards the rumpled bed with Ari's legs still wrapped around her and their tongues slow dancing from one mouth to the other. She laid Ari back on the bed and sat back to straddle her hips. She watched the eyes watching her as she unbuttoned her cufflinks and pulled her shirt free from her pants. She peeled it off her shoulders and tossed it to the floor behind her. Her satin bra was quick to follow revealing small, round breasts, slightly broad shoulders, and faint lines of the muscles in her abdomen. Rian leaned forward pressing her breasts to Ari's and pinning her hands above her head. She teased her lips with her tongue and pulled away just to make Ari chase her before passionately kissing her again. She loved the feel of her lips so much she could sometimes climax just from kissing her.

Ari groaned and pushed her hips up into Rian. Their kissing drove her crazy she needed more. Rian pulled back from the kiss and bent her head lower sucking a nipple between her lips and biting the tip with her teeth. She repeated the same motion with the other breast, then licked and sucked them until they were hard and standing at attention like pink erasers.

"Please, baby." Ari moved her hips again. "Rian, I need you." Her voice had taken on a slightly husky tone.

Rian let her hands go and rocked against her as she sat up. Ari went to work unbuttoning Rian's pants. She slipped her hand inside and ran her fingers through the swollen folds finding the silky wet spot that drove Rian crazy. When Rian bucked against the fingers teasing her she quickly moved to the side and pushed her pants off, then covered Ari's naked body with her own. She loved the way Ari's smooth, soft skin felt against her. She bent her head and met her lips for another heart-stopping kiss that nearly sent her over the edge when Ari sucked her tongue into her mouth.

When Ari's hips moved under her, Rian reached down with one hand and ran her fingers in lazy circles around her clit teasing her entrance with each pass. Ari moved in rhythm with her.

"Yes baby," she panted between kisses. "I want to feel you inside me when I come."

Rian slipped two fingers inside and continued the circles around her clit with her thumb pushing her fingers deeper with each thrust. Ari dug her short nails into Rian's back and pressed her heels into the bed for leverage as her body began to tighten. Rian kissed her softly and stroked her gently as her climax subsided.

"I love you so much," Ari said when her breathing finally slowed. Rian looked into the green and blue eyes staring up at her and ran her clean hand across her cheek.

"You make my life complete, Ari. I don't know what I'd ever do without you," Rian said just before she kissed her one last time. Then, she rolled away and stood up.

"Where are you going?" Ari raised an eyebrow.

"To take another shower and get my ass to work," she said walking across the room. She turned around when she heard another pair of bare feet on the hardwood floor. "Can I help you?" She teased.

"No, but I can help you," Ari said pushing Rian back against the wall and bent down on her knees. She ran her hands up Rian's legs from her ankles to the top her thighs and spread them. She smiled when she saw the glisten wet folds between the thin patch of dark hair. She looked up at the smoky eyes watching her as she slid her tongue across the folds with enough pressure to roll her clit back and forth. She held Rian tightly against the wall and used her thumbs to spread her open even further. She ran her tongue in circles then sucked her clit into her mouth over and over again as Rian's hips moved against. When she pushed her tongue inside Rian reached down and put her hand in Ari's hair on the back of her head and held Ari's face against her throbbing center.

"Suck me baby," she said between gasps.

Ari moved one hand and slid two fingers inside of Rian and sucked her clit at the same time alternating thrusts and sucks until she felt Rian's hand tighten in her hair just enough to cause her to suck harder and thrust deeper. Rian came wildly against her face.

When she caught her breath she reached down and pulled Ari to her feet. "You amaze me,"

"You didn't think I was going to let you go all day like that did you?" Ari said with a smile as she wrapped her arms around Rian's neck and pressed her body against her. Rian kissed her tasting herself on her lips and tongue. That fanned the flames, making her want to do it all over again.

"I guess you better get in the shower with me or I am never going to go to work today," Rian grinned.

Chapter Two

Rian was sitting at her desk reading the latest Intel reports on the one subject that had taken up most of the last year and half of her life. She was assigned to the South American Organized Crime Division and taking down an Argentinean Crime Boss named Fiorino Canturri was her main objective. Canturri had been smuggling guns into the United States for a number of years. They were being sold on the streets in the black markets and he was also funding various South American terrorist cells. Rian was building a case that was already two inches thick with reports from informants, satellite photos, offshore bank transactions, and boxes of weapons that were traced to South America. She wasn't sloppy. She'd done her homework and made sure her T's were crossed and her I's were dotted. She was looking forward to the day she could have him extradited to the states to answer for the crimes he committed and the hundreds if not thousands of lives that had been lost due to his crimes. Rian made a few notes in the file from the new Intel and locked the file in her briefcase. It wasn't a matter of trust. It was more like a habit that she hid her files from everyone and took everything with her when she left for any reason. Of course, she had back up files on her laptop, but again that went everywhere with her too.

"How's it coming, Agent Casey? Are we any closer to nailing this rat bastard?" Section Chief Philip Walsh was standing in the doorway to her tiny cubicle office. He was physically fit and average height with receding salt and pepper hair. Rian knew him as a colleague and respected him when he became her superior just after she was promoted to the senior agent on to this case.

"Yes, I was just reading the latest satellite reports. It looks like he may have a shipment moving out soon. His guys have been extremely busy with trucks coming and going from the compound. This matches the recent account transactions. If I could tie those accounts to him personally, I'd be really close," she said.

"Good, good," he nodded. "Keep me informed. We need to have everything in line when we present the evidence for the extradition warrant." He turned to walk away, but turned back towards her. "We missed you at the briefing meeting this morning," he said.

"Car trouble," she said. "I need to trade my unmarked in for one of our ceased vehicles before the damn thing leaves me stranded one day."

He nodded and sipped his coffee. "Go pick one out of the line this afternoon and get the paperwork on my desk before the day is over. I don't need my agents missing important meetings."

~

Ari walked through the doors of the condo building and looked around for Rian's car. They had dinner reservations at a small Italian restaurant that had authentic Italian cuisine and a romantic atmosphere. It was one of their favorite places and an easy choice for their anniversary dinner. Ari had just hung up the phone with Rian and knew she had arrived, but the car in her usual parking spot wasn't the black unmarked she drove.

Rian saw Ari standing on the curb in a short, spaghetti strap black dress. She ran her eyes down her body from her long wavy hair twisted up in a clip, down her slim hour-glass figure, to her smooth, tan legs and black low-heeled strappy sandals. She felt her chest tighten and her crotch dampen at the sight of the beautiful woman. She smiled as she watched Ari eyeing the suspicious car and looking around for her at the same time. She saw her jump when she finally flashed the headlights. Then, she powered down the window and waved. Ari's brows rose and she walked towards the silver four-door Audi shaking her head.

"Who did you steal this from?" She said when she got in. She adjusted her short dress on the black leather seat and leaned across the console to meet Rian's lips in a fierce kiss.

Rian pulled back breathlessly and grinned. "This is because of my 'car trouble' this morning."

Ari raised an eyebrow. "What…" Then it hit her and she smiled from ear to ear. "I see."

"I missed a briefing and Walsh was riding my ass. When I told him I had trouble with my unmarked he signed me out with this. Enjoy it while it lasts. I doubt he realizes he gave me the best car in our ceased fleet. He'd probably take it for himself if he knew about it," she said as she ran her hand from Ari's knee up her thigh and under the bottom of her dress. She knew Ari wouldn't stop her. She was more inclined to lean back and spread her legs. That was one of the things Rian loved about her; she was so carefree and lived life to the fullest every day. Rian brushed her fingers over the front of the lace thong between Ari's legs and leaned over to kiss her again before pulling away completely.

"You better finish what you started later," Ari said.

"I can't wait," Rian teased as she threw the car in reverse and rolled out of the parking spot. She was barely in drive when her foot stomped the gas in the heady sports car throwing Ari slightly back in her seat as she buckled her safety belt.

"I see you're enjoying this little toy."

"Oh baby, you have no idea. I've been driving all over today. I had a few important errands to run and I had a meeting in Quantico. You should feel this thing on the highway," Rian's face lit-up like a small child. Ari shook her head and smiled.

~

Rian and Ari had a small private table in the back of the dimly lit restaurant. They had only drunk half of their bottle of wine by the time they were finished with their dinner. Rian told the waiter to take the remainder of the expensive bottle home to share with his girlfriend.

"That was nice of you. You're such a sweetheart, Rian. I think that's why I love you so much," Ari said squeezing her hand.

"You make me that way you know. Before you, I pretty much kept to myself. How many times did I come into the coffee shop before asking you out? At least a hundred," she smiled.

Ari laughed softly. "I don't think it was quite that many, but it was a lot. I remember thinking you were as hot as the coffee I was serving you and I was so scared I was going to mess up and drop it, or spill it on you or something."

"I miss going in there and seeing you every day," Rian said.

"I miss seeing you in the middle of your day, but I definitely don't miss being a barista. Besides, working in the fashion world suits me much better. Don't you think?" She waved her hands over herself.

"You were beautiful when I met you and you look gorgeous tonight. You could be wearing a t-shirt and sweatpants and I'd think you were sexy, you know that," she said with a smile. "I just want you to do whatever makes you happy."

"You make me happy, Rian. You and only you, I'll never be able to tell you how much I love you or how much you've changed my life."

"How about I show you how much you've changed mine." Rian stood up from her chair and knelt on one knee next to Ari. She pulled a small velvet bag from the inside pocket of her jacket and slipped a shiny platinum ring with two small diamonds and one large center diamond into her hand. Ari gasped when Rian held the ring between her fingers and presented it to her. "I love you so much, Ari Turner. Please say you will marry me," Rian reached up and wiped the tears from Ari's face with her free hand.

"Oh Rian, oh my…yes. Yes I want nothing more than to spend the rest of my life with you," she said. She held her left hand out so Rian could place the ring on her finger. She was still crying and Rian wondered if maybe she'd made a mistake.

"Are you okay?" She asked as she got up and wrapped her arms around Ari. Most of the restaurant was closed off to them, but the few people close by were clapping for them.

"Yes," Ari wiped the remainder of the tears away. "I'm just surprised. That's all."

"We don't have to do anything soon. The length of our engagement is at your discretion. Just let me know when and where and I'll be standing next to you ready to give you the rest of my life," Rian kissed her softly and pulled her to her feet. "Let's get out of here. I'd much rather be naked in bed with you right now."

They walked out of the restaurant hand in hand. Rian leaned over to whisper in Ari's ear just as a loud pop sounded in the distance. She immediately went for the gun under her jacket as a car sped off. She had no idea anyone had been hit until she realized Ari was no longer next to her. She turned around to see Ari lying on the side of the curb with the front of her black dress soaking through.

"Oh god no!" she yelled as she dropped to her knees next to Ari and cradled her head against her. "Someone call an ambulance!" she screamed and took her jacket off and pressed it to the bleeding wound in the middle of Ari's chest just below her breasts. "Please hold on, baby. It'll be okay, Ari, I promise. Just don't leave me. Please god, don't take her from me," Rian cried.

Ari was barely breathing and her eyes fluttered back and forth. "I'll always love you, Rian," she whispered.

Numerous people standing around tried to help her, but she told them not to touch Ari. There was nothing they could really do anyway, unless they were doctors. She quickly fumbled around her neck trying to find a pulse, but felt nothing.

"No…no…don't do this to me, Ari. Come on." She checked again, but there was nothing. She opened her eyelids and only saw pupils staring blankly past her. "NO! Damn it you come back to me, Ari," she cried and held her body tightly against her.

When the EMT's finally arrived they had to pry Rian away to get a look at Ari. The two young men felt for a pulse and didn't find one either. They tried CPR for two minutes and decided to pronounce her dead.

"No, you have to save her," Rian said from nearby. "Isn't there something in that bag or that god damn truck

15

that will bring her back?" she yelled as she wiped the tears away but they kept falling.

"I'm sorry, ma'am," one of the EMT's said to her. Just to be certain, they put leads on Ari's chest and hooked her up to a portable EKG monitor and when it came on the line was completely flat. She was gone.

Two Washington D.C. police officers tried to assist Rian as she watched them load Ari's body into the ambulance and drive off without the lights and siren. She could barely stand. When the ambulance was out of sight she turned around. Her suit jacket was in a heap on the blood stained curb.

"Is there someone we can call for you, Agent Casey?" one of the officers asked. "Or can we take you to the hospital, or maybe take you home?"

Rian just stared at the large red spot on the white-ash colored sidewalk. She knelt down and put her hand next to the spot subconsciously checking to see if the ground was still warm, looking for some connection to the woman that only minutes ago was smiling in her arms. She folded her legs Indian style and stayed right there next to the spot where Ari laid dying in her arms.

The officers cleared the crowd away as the local detectives arrived. They tried to question Rian, but she was so distraught she could barely tell them her name. One of the officers got her ID out of her jacket when he saw it on the ground just after he arrived. He gave it to the lead detective.

Ten minutes later, Philip Walsh pushed through the crowd with his badge in the air. He spoke to the detective to let him know he had a crew on the way that would take over the case since this was considered a code-blue where one of their own was down. He also retrieved her ID badge before walking over to Rian.

"We need to get you out of here, Agent Casey," he said as he bent down next to her. "Come on, let's get you home."

She looked up at him with a blank stare. Her smoky gray eyes were almost solid black and the tears were starting to dry on her face. Walsh unstrapped her gun from its holster under her arm and tucked it into the back of his pants. She never even felt him touch her as he put his arms under hers and lifted her to her feet. He held her against him as he felt around her pockets for her car keys.

"Can I get one of you officers to follow me in her car, thanks," he said as he practically carried her to his car. He was thankful he had all of his agent's home addresses programmed into the GPS on his phone. He never thought he'd need to access that file.

He drove through the dark streets of Washington D.C., passing the Capitol and other monuments in silence. When he first got the call he thought one of his agents had been gunned down. It took him a second to realize it was Agent Casey's girlfriend. He'd only met Ari once or twice when she came to the office to have lunch with Rian in the restaurant that took up the entire first floor of their building. He didn't really know what to say to her. He'd prepared the speech in his head a hundred times in case he ever had to go tell a wife that her husband was killed in the line of duty. Somehow, that speech didn't fit this situation and he was lost for words. The ghost of a person sitting next to him wasn't helping much. He wondered if maybe he should have taken her to the hospital to get evaluated.

When they arrived at her condo building he thanked the officers for helping him out. They offered to help him get her inside, but he had it under control. He checked the file in his phone for her address again. She was in number five-one-five. He looked around for the elevator. Rian was looking more and more ghastly and hollow. She was no help. Finally, he heard the ding coming from around the corner. He gathered her against him and walked in that direction. The doors opened on the top floor which was the fifth floor and he followed the signs leading to the fifteenth apartment. He fumbled with her keys and opened the door. It was pitch black inside. He left her in the hallway and drew his weapon. He walked inside feeling each wall for the light switches as he cleared the two bedroom loft style apartment one room at a time. As soon as he cleared the apartment and everything was secure he went back into the hallway, brought her inside, and sat her down on the couch.

Philip Walsh had never been in this sort of situation and had no idea what to say or do to try and ease her pain. Instead, he went to the tiny bar in the dining area and poured two glasses of the golden brown liquid in the crystal decanter. He handed one to Rian when he sat down next to her and placed his own glass on the coffee table in front of them. He watched as Rian wiped away silent tears as she took a couple of long swallows. She never looked at him and hadn't said a single word since he arrived at the crime scene. He knew she was in shock and thought about calling one of the psychologists that they worked with to get some advice on how to help her with this grief, but his cell phone rang changing his mind for him.

"Walsh," he said when he answered it.

"We just wrapped the crime scene that involved Agent Casey," a deep male voice said from the other end of the line. "We recovered one shell casing, looks like maybe a .223 caliber. The only witnesses said the vehicle was a dark SUV. Two people said maybe a Chevy Tahoe or Trailblazer, one person said it was a Ford Explorer, and another person said it looked like a Cadillac Escalade. So, we have no vehicle to go on and a spent shell casing isn't a whole hell of a lot."

"Well, keep looking. Turn every stone if you have to. The local detective that was on scene said it looked like a through and through so make sure you check the building structure, parked vehicles, anything the bullet could be stuck in. Contact the hospital in the morning and see if the autopsy has been completed, this case is top priority. I'll make some calls when the sun comes up to make sure the medical examiner knows this is a 'code blue'. Update me if anything else comes up," he said before he hung up. Rian was still sitting next to him, her glass was empty and he noticed the one in front of him was empty too.

"I'm very sorry for you loss, Rian. We will do everything we can to catch whoever did this," he said as he stood up. "Call me if you need anything. I'll check in with you tomorrow. You're on bereavement status until further notice."

Special Agent Walsh was already riding the elevator to the bottom floor when the heavy crystal glass smashed against the door. Rian sobbed uncontrollably when she looked up at the pictures hanging on the wall across from her. Ari was smiling down at her with the light from the lamp dancing over her uniquely beautiful eyes. Her mind raced back to the last second she saw her alive lying in her arms bleeding out, she wasn't smiling and her eyes were closed. The contrast made her sick to her stomach. She jumped up and hurried to the bathroom down the hall barely making it before she began hurling.

There was no telling how long she puked, or how long the dry heaves lasted. She must have blacked out because she woke up on the cold tile floor. It was still dark outside and her cheeks were wet with fresh tears. Rian splashed cold water on her face. She walked back into the living room, poured another glass of whiskey and sat on the couch.

~

The next day Philip Walsh showed up at lunchtime with a pizza. Rian was still wearing the same clothes when she opened the door. He noticed the smashed glass on the floor crunching under his feet when he walked in. He also noticed the second glass still sitting on the table in front the couch and the whiskey level in the decanter on the other side of the room was much lower than when he left the night before. He set the pizza on the dining room table and swept the glass up with a broom and dustpan he found in the kitchen.

"You should probably eat something," he said nodding towards the pizza. Rian just stared blankly at him. He wished she had family for him to call, but he'd been through her file twice in the past few hours and she had very few members listed and they were all in California, so they wouldn't really be much good to her right now. Besides, he had no idea if they even knew about her private life. He only knew because he'd been introduced to Ari, otherwise Rian pretty much kept her private life private. FBI agents were trained to be reclusive, the less that was known about them the better.

"Call me if you need anything," he said as moved towards the door.

Rian lie on the couch and curled in a ball as more tears fell. She had no idea how to talk anymore. She felt like her mind shut completely down. She wanted to die too, anything to make the hurting stop. Her head was pounding so hard she could barely see, her stomach was cramping and burning from drinking only aged whiskey and throwing it back up a few times over, and her chest ached with heavy pressure that felt like someone was squishing her to death slowly. For all she knew it could have been a heart attack, but her mind was so blank she'd surely die before she figured it out if that's what it was. She was mad at Ari for leaving her, then mad at herself for being mad at Ari, followed by a deep sadness that completely contained her and controlled her mind, body, and soul. Every time she closed her eyes she saw her dying body lying in the puddle of blood and every time she was asleep she felt her lifeless body in her arms. Both instances were causing her to relive it all over again.

Chapter Three

Three days had passed since the fatal drive by shooting that took Ari's life. Rian drank a half gallon of water and ate the two day old pizza that somehow made it into the refrigerator. She finally took the dirty clothes off that she'd been wearing since that night. She threw the bloodstained garments into the trash and forced herself not to look at the rumpled bed sheets as she grabbed a clean suit from the closet and her toiletries from the bathroom. She stood under the hot spray of the shower in the spare bathroom. The tight, tense muscles in her back started to relax slowly as she scrubbed three days worth of human stench from her skin and shampooed the greasy dirt from her short hair.

Special Agent Philip Walsh was surprised to hear Rian's voice when his phone rang early that morning. She sounded hollow, almost weak, but he understood why she was getting out of the house. She didn't want to be there in the first place everything was a reminder of the life left behind, a life that died with Ari on that sidewalk. He wondered if he could pick up the pieces of his life in only a few days if he ever experienced that kind of devastation. He told her the name of the hospital that

Ari's body had been taken to. As far as he knew, it was still there in the morgue waiting to be claimed by family and sent to a funeral home. She told him she was Ari's only family so more than likely it was there waiting for her. She felt cold talking about Ari as an inanimate object.

It had been three very long days since Rian had seen the sun. She felt like the bright rays were going to blind her eyes hidden behind dark sunglasses. She stared at the green Toyota Camry parked in the spot next to the empty one her unmarked use to occupy. She took a deep breath and held back the tears threatening to fall. She needed to be strong, there were arrangements that needed to be handled and calls that had to be made. Ari had no family. Her parents died when she was young and she finished her teenage years with her grandmother who passed just before Rian and Ari started dating. Rian had no idea what her final wishes were. Who thinks about that kind of thing at twenty-eight years old? Rian was thirty-three and didn't even have a will of her own.

Sitting behind the wheel of the Audi sports sedan brought that fateful night right back to her. She was screwed either way. She had two options, drive the Audi or Ari's Camry. She put her safety belt on and turned the key. With one final glance to the left she reversed out of the parking spot and sped off.

~

Rian's nose wrinkled when she walked into the hospital morgue. She'd been in morgues and seen dead bodies more times than she'd care to admit during her career, but nothing ever prepared her for the way she would react to walking in there knowing it was Ari's body she was going to see. She quickly stepped back out and hurried down the hall towards the restroom sign. The bile rose in her throat before she could get to an open stall so she puked in the sink. When the dry heaves finally stopped she moved to the other sink and rinsed her mouth and splashed cold water on her face. It mixed with warm salty tears as it ran down her cheeks and off her chin. She dried her hands and face on a paper towel that felt more like sand paper on her delicate skin. She casually looked under the stalls before standing up and adjusting her suit jacket thankful no one else was in there with her. She looked at herself one more time in the mirror before walking back to the morgue.

"Can I help you?" An older man in light green scrubs and a white lab coat walked over to her. His hair was thinning on the sides and his head was bald on top and shining in the bright lights.

"I'm here to claim the body of a family member so I can have it sent to a funeral home," she said as she swallowed the lump in her throat.

He pressed a few keys in the laptop sitting on the table. "What's the name of the deceased?"

"Ari Turner,"

"I don't see that name here. Are you sure the body was brought here?" he questioned.

"Yes. She was shot Tuesday night and was DOA. I'm an FBI agent and I was told by my Agent in Charge that her body was brought here. I'm her only family so I'm sure she hasn't been claimed," she sighed and showed him her ID badge.

"I don't remember seeing her, but as medical examiners we generally float to all of the hospitals." He typed a few more keys. "Here it is. Ari Turner was transferred into the custody of Capital Funeral Home on Wednesday. I'm not familiar with the M.E. on her record, but as I said anyone could have handled her case. It says here she was DOA with a high caliber gunshot wound. The bullet appeared to have entered the upper quadrant of the torso and exited to the right of the spinal cord. There was not a full autopsy completed."

Rian took in everything he was saying. Ari had no chance to live through that kind of wound. Her chest was tight and aching thinking of the pain Ari must have felt as she slowly bled out in her arms. She cleared her throat and choked back tears. "Excuse me did you say the body was transferred to a funeral home?"

"Yes, ma'am," he looked at the screen. "Capital Funeral Home."

"How can a body be sent to a funeral home if it hasn't been claimed by a family member?" she asked.

"Sometimes family members don't come here to claim their relatives. If the body has been positively identified by a driver's license or other means such as finger prints or law enforcement verification then whatever funeral home they chose calls and we release the body to them for transfer. I'm not sure how she was identified, that information is not in her record." He simply stated.

Rian nodded and thanked him. She didn't quite understand their philosophy, but she was at a dead end literally so she headed off in the direction of the funeral home. She knew this process would be difficult, but she never realized it would be so draining. Her body felt like she was carrying around a lead weight around her neck.

Rian reached the other side of town rather quickly in the mid-morning traffic and parked in front of the large building. A tall black man in a dark suit and tie greeted her when she walked inside. He reminded her of a fellow agent with his stiff demeanor and 'Men in Black' attire.

"I was just told by a member of the morgue staff at Washington Hospital Center that my relative's body was sent here. I need to verify that please," she showed him her ID Badge. "Her name is Ari Turner. She was transferred here on Wednesday, I believe."

He led her towards a small office where he sat behind the desk and started typing on the computer. He stopped and looked at her, then typed a few more keys. "Ari Turner, you said?"

"Yes,"

He typed some more keys. "We received a written order to retrieve her body on Wednesday for general cremation. Her ashes are currently waiting to be picked up," he said when he looked up at her.

"Excuse me?" she said.

"She was cremated yesterday according to our records we had a signed order to retrieve the body from

27

Washington Hospital Center Wednesday morning and go ahead with general cremation which is usually completed within twenty-four hours," he said.

"Wait a minute," Rian was trying to wrap her head around the fact that they cremated her body without her knowing. Who approved all of this? I'm her next of kin and I damn sure didn't tell you to do this."

"It says here her Power of Attorney authorized everything. His name is Wilfred Bonamy. He faxed over the signed forms. This is very common with estates. Sometimes the family attorney is the person handling the final arrangements for the family if there are no family members named in the Will or Power of Attorney."

"I see. So this Wilfred person said he was her Power of Attorney and that authorized him to make the decisions regarding her funeral? Is this correct?" she asked.

He stood up and walked over to the filing cabinet and pulled a file out. "Here are the forms he faxed us. I don't know if I'm even supposed to show you these, but you're FBI so you can get them if you want them I guess," he handed her a few pages. "This is her signed Power of Attorney with her Driver's License attached. All of the signatures matched. There's no reason we would question these documents."

Rian's chest burned when she saw Ari looking back at her in the photo on the copy of her driver's license. She turned the page quickly. He was right, the documents were legal. She did notice the date they were signed was two months before they started dating. That's why Rian's name wasn't on them. Ari probably never thought about changing them. Most people write a Will or designate a Power of Attorney and forget all about it. There was also a copy of Ari's Will which stated she wanted to be cremated and forgotten. That line made Rian cringe. It didn't sound like the Ari she knew that was so full of life. She was like a butterfly that emerged from a cocoon over the two years they were together. She was no longer that shy young woman Ari met in the coffee shop. She wondered what would make her want to be forgotten. Maybe it was the sadness of not having any family. Rian vowed to make her remembered, not forgotten.

She sighed. "Well, obviously this was written and signed before she and I started dating two years ago and she forgot to change it. I never knew about it," she handed the papers back to him.

"I'm sorry," he said.

"It's not your fault. May I please take her ashes with me?"

"Uh, I need to check on that. I'm not sure if the Power of Attorney needs to authorize that or not."

"Do you have his contact information? I'll call him from here and he can fax you whatever you need."

He opened the file again and handed her the top page that had his law office phone number and address on the top. He waited while she used his desk phone.

"Hi, this is Senior Special Agent Rian Casey with the FBI. Can I please speak with Wilfred Bonamy please?"

"This is he," a deep male voice answered. "How may I help you, Agent?"

"I'm in a bit of a situation. One of your clients named Ari Turner was my partner of two years and fiancé actually when she passed away this week. I was unaware of the Will and Power of Attorney you provided to Capital Funeral Home. It appears to have been drawn up and signed just before we began dating and she probably forgot about it over the last couple of years," she paused.

"I'm sorry for your loss, Agent Casey. I had no idea. The day she came into my office she wanted everything drawn up right then. I typed it up, she signed it, and I never saw her again. She said she had no family and wanted everything to be quick and hassle-free when she passed. She even paid for the fees upfront. I thought it was a little strange coming from such a young person, but she mentioned her parents passed at a young age and she had a feeling she would too."

Rian wiped a stray tear. Ari was such a broken person when she met her and she never knew it. Ari was shy at first, but soon she opened up and blossomed into this amazingly happy, beautiful woman. "She definitely forgot about that part of her life I'm sure. If you could have seen her recently, Mr. Bonamy, you'd think we were talking about two different people. She was vibrant and so full of life."

"I'm very sorry. She was definitely taken way too soon."

"Yes she was," She sighed and regained her thoughts. "I would like to have her ashes and the funeral home needs a faxed consent form since you're her Power of Attorney."

"Oh that's no problem. I will fax the release as soon as we hang up. Again, I'm sorry for your loss. Please let me know if I can assist you with anything else," he said before hanging up.

Rian waited and watched the fax machine come to life a few minutes later. The man behind the desk nodded and added the form to Ari's file.

"I'll be right back," he said.

She couldn't believe the events of the morning. She was still shocked that Ari's body had been cremated without her being involved. She wondered how much more she didn't know about her. She turned her head when she heard the office door open. The tall black man walked in with a basic metal vase with a sealed lid. Ari's name and dates of birth and death were etched on the front. She almost dropped it when he handed it to her. She wasn't expecting it to be so heavy. She rubbed the side the same way she used to rub Ari's cheek with the back of her fingers. He handed her a tissue when he saw the tears rolling down her cheeks.

"Thanks," she whispered as she wiped her face. "Is there anything else I need to do?"

"Just print your name here and sign on that line." He pointed to the two spots. She quickly printed and signed her name and left the building before she lost it in front of him. She strapped the vase into the passenger seat next to her so it didn't go rolling around. It was ironic the last time Ari was in that car she was alive and happy, only to die an hour and a half later. Now, she was in the same seat of the car again, only dead and reduced to ashes.

Rian shook her head and forced herself to breathe. She wanted to die too, this was just too hard. She couldn't remember her life before Ari and nothing made her want to live it without her. She rested her forehead on the steering wheel and cried until the tears stopped. Of all places to break down a funeral home was probably the most common, but it still felt odd. She looked over at the shiny capped vase.

"I love you so damn much," she whispered as she rubbed the side.

When she finally composed herself again she drove home and placed Ari's ashes up on the mantel next to the last picture they took together at Constitution Gardens, a beautiful lake spot at the National Mall between the Washington Monument and Lincoln Memorial. They met there in that same spot often for picnic lunches. Ari loved looking at the historical buildings and watching the ducks in the lake.

Chapter Four

Rian watched the orange spread across the sky kissing everything in its path as the sun rose slowly over trees surrounding the Potomac River. She was sitting on the wrought iron bench in the park she and Ari often visited. It had been two long days since she picked Ari's ashes up from the funeral home and only five days since the night she died in Rian's arms on that cold sidewalk.

The shiny urn sat on the bench next to her. Rian wiped the tears from her cheeks. Ari's small private service was scheduled for eight a.m. and she arrived early to silently say her goodbyes to the woman that made her want to live. Ironically, all she made her want to do now was die.

"I'd give anything to be with you right now, where ever you are." she said as she ran the back of her hand over the capped vase. "I'll always love you, Ari, you and only you." she wiped more tears and cleared her throat.

A few of Ari's old colleagues and friends from the coffee shop arrived for the service, followed by Philip Walsh and a few other agents that often worked with Rian on various cases. Rian welcomed them with a thin smile and clammy hands.

At precisely eight o'clock a bald, light-skinned, black man dressed in a dark suit like Rian and the other agents wore stepped up next the small stand Ari's urn and picture were sitting on. His deep voice rumbled when he spoke.

"I didn't have the pleasure of knowing this beautiful young woman, Ari Turner, but her partner in life, Rian Casey is a Senior Special Agent with the Federal Bureau of Investigation and a colleague. For those of you that do not know me or haven't had the unfortunate circumstances that render my services, my name is Dewayne Montgomery. I officiate government clerical services. I was asked by Agent Casey to perform the service today for her beloved partner Ari Turner.

I spent a few hours yesterday afternoon with Rian getting to know Ari through her and one of the things that really stood out in our conversation was Ari's happiness. Rian stated many times how generally happy she always was and she loved living life. It didn't matter what she was doing she always had a smile on her face. Rian told me about how they first met in a small coffee shop over two years ago and it took Rian a number of months to get the courage up to ask her out. Ari was shy and sort of reclusive and almost declined the offer, but something happened the first time Rian and Ari's hands touched. Maybe it was fate or divine intervention, but Rian said she looked into Ari's unique eyes and fell in love for the first time in her life. She silently vowed at that moment to spend the rest of her life with this beautiful, amazing woman," he paused and looked at Rian.

"Who would've thought it would be the rest of Ari's life they would be spending together. They spent two wonderful, happy years together. Sadly, the night Ari was taken from this world they got engaged and were looking forward to many more happy years together. Rian said Ari passed with a smile on her face. Even in death she was happy," he said just before leading a prayer that Ari was where she was supposed to be and he asked God to look down and watch over Rian during her grieving and help her understand and get through the process using the happy times and memories they shared together.

When he was finished Rian took his place. She picked the urn up and held it to her chest. "Ari, wherever you are, you'll never know how much you changed my life. You were my rock, my whole world. In life people say everything happens for a reason and I will never know the reason you were taken away from me. I keep waiting for you to step out from behind something and walk up to me with that sweet smile on your face," she wiped tears from her face and cleared her throat.

"I'll never again have the life I had with you. I can't tell myself you're in a better place because to me there was no better place to be than with you. I'll never let you go, Ari. I've loved you since the day I asked you to have dinner with me and I'll continue to love you for the rest of my life," she sniffed and wiped more tears as she turned and walked towards the flowing river. "This was our happy place. You loved coming here and I couldn't think of a more fitting place to let you rest."

Rian took the lid off the urn and knelt down towards the water. "Goodbye, my love," she said as she poured the ashes into the water and watched them float away before sinking. She set the empty vase next to her and sat back in the grass as she cried uncontrollable. A few of Ari's old work friends walked up to try and console her as their own tears fell, but Dewayne Montgomery waved everyone away and sat down next to her.

They sat in silence for over an hour as ducks swam by. Rian cried until her tears were dry while she stared blankly at the water flowing in front of her. She was empty, no feeling, no pain, not even sadness. She was just plain lost. What was left of her soul floated away with Ari's ashes.

"I'm here if you want to talk," Dewayne said as he put his hand on her shoulder. "No one understands what you are going through, they never will. Every relationship is different, just like every person is different. I can only tell you I was in similar shoes ten years ago when my wife died of cancer. She was diagnosed and died twelve weeks later. It was very sudden and like you I was devastated. That's why I became a member of the clergy and stayed with the Bureau," he turned around when he heard footsteps in the grass. Section Chief Philip Walsh was standing a few feet away.

"It looks like someone wants to talk to you. Take care of yourself, Rian, and know I am always here if you ever want to talk, need to vent, whatever. I understand."

Dewayne shook his head when he passed by and Walsh asked if she was okay. He wasn't sure what to say to her. He couldn't get the image of finding her on the curb covered in blood out of his head. He felt sorry for her as he knelt down and put a hand on her shoulder.

"I can't begin to find words that make any sense, so I'm just going to say take as much time as you feel you need. I will hold your gun and badge until you're ready to come back. We are a family at the bureau and when one of our family members needs us we are there for him or her. So, if there is anything I can do just let me know," he stood up and turned to walk away before turning back to her. "Do you need help getting home?"

Rian continued to silently stare straight ahead and shook her head slightly to the side. She never moved as he walked away quietly. The funeral guests were long gone and the park was starting to fill up with picnic goers and joggers.

Chapter Five

Two long, agonizing weeks had gone by since she sat on that grassy riverbank as her soul died and floated away with Ari's ashes. Rian drank more whiskey than she ever thought her body could tolerate, but it helped or at least she felt like it did. She spent most of time packing up the apartment one box at a time. She didn't want to be there if Ari wasn't there. They moved there together and it just wasn't home anymore without her. She'd also spent countless hours trying to decide what to do with the rest of her life. She forgot what it was like being alone and everything in and around Washington, D.C. reminded her of a life she didn't want anymore.

Rian was lost in thought when the door opened and Philip Walsh stepped out and waved her inside his office. He was glad to see her, but he honestly thought she might take another week or two after the way she appeared at the funeral. He'd never personally watched someone grieve and hoped he never did it again.

"It's good to see you, Agent Casey. How are you doing?" he asked.

She took a deep breath and pulled a white envelope from the inside pocket of her jacket and slid it across the desk.

"What's this?" he said as he began to open it.

"It's my resignation, effective immediately." she said.

He tore the envelope open and read it quickly. "Rian, don't do this. Don't throw your career away, you're still grieving. Give it some time."

"I've had more than enough time, sir. I'm done."

"I wish you wouldn't do this. You're one of my best agents. Hell, Rian, you and I worked together on hundreds of cases before I took this position. I know you, you love being an agent."

"What I *love* is no longer here." she said with a little more force than needed.

"Your record is exemplary. You will get full retirement honors upon completion of your resignation." She shrugged and shook his hand.

He slid the letter back into the envelope. "I'll hold onto this for a few more weeks in case you change your mind."

Rian nodded and walked away.

~

A month later, Special Agent Philip Walsh received the call he was never expecting. Sure, he knew Rian Casey would go back to work eventually. Even when he completed her resignation paperwork three weeks before he knew one day she would move on. He was happy to hear that had happened, he wasn't happy however to hear she was taking a job with the Portland Police Department as a Cold Case Detective. She had obviously given up on life and on herself. At one time she was on top as a senior special agent with the FBI and looking at a promotion down the road if she continued on that same path. Now, she was barely staying afloat and doing someone else's bullshit work.

Walsh gave the glowing recommendation he promised her when she resigned. He was sorry to see where it went though. He shook his head when he hung up the phone. In a way, he felt very sorry for her, but he wished her good luck and went back to the case notes he was reading before the phone rang.

Chapter Six

Rian was going through the motions of life one day at a time reading through one cold case file at a time. She spent her days calling old witnesses and searching for new leads while her nights were spent tossing and turning and occasionally drowning in the bottle. The fire in her gut and light her eyes had long ago burned out. She simply existed.

When she ran across a strange case that sounded vaguely familiar it reminded her of a case she partially worked involving a serial killer during one of her early years with the bureau. The cold case she was currently reading had many similarities that caught her attention. She quickly wrote as many notes as she could about the case she had worked and took off down the hall towards Captain Burke's office.

Captain Malcolm Burke respected Rian for being an FBI agent, but he was surprised to hear the commendation she got from the bureau and respect they had for her as an agent. All he saw in her was a cold, lonely shell of a person that kept to herself. He often wondered what her story was, but he couldn't deny the recommendation, so he hired her on the spot.

"Captain, I ran across this homicide from three years ago, a middle-aged woman was randomly shot in broad daylight by a high-powered rifle at a long distance and left for dead in the street," she flipped through the file. "Her name was Hillenbrand, Monica Hillenbrand."

"What about it? Did you find a new lead?" he asked.

"Well, not necessarily. I worked on a case in my second or third year with the bureau that was similar. There was a serial killer named Jacob Perry that was randomly shooting people from building rooftops all over Illinois. I believe he was using a hunting rifle. He'd been a sniper or sharp shooter I think in the Army at one time. Anyway, over the course of a year he picked off at least a dozen people in the state before we were able to catch him."

"How are these cases linked?"

"I'm not sure if they're linked, but there are similarities. Also, it was never proven, but there were rumors that Perry had an apprentice, a person to take his place if he got caught. It's possible, if that's true, this person could be continuing Jacob Perry's hunting spree. I would need to do some more research and see if I can find anymore similar cases."

Captain Burke leaned back in his desk chair causing it to squeak loudly. He pursed his lips and folded his hands. "So you think a serial killer's assistant or whatever, is killing people on the other side of the country ten years later? Is that correct?"

Rian knew she was a highly trained investigator and could easily prove her point, but she didn't care anymore, not about the job, not about anything. "It's just a hunch, a similarity that I thought I would bring to your attention. Do whatever you want with it." She stood up and walked out of his office and back to her tiny metal desk in the cold case file room at the end of the hallway. She wondered why he had even hired her. It's not like they actually had a position for a strictly 'cold case' detective. She figured maybe she was put on the payroll due to her skills and put on cold cases as sort a holding pattern until she was actually needed. She decided to search the cold cases and pull aside any random shooting cases to put together a profile on her own time. If this really was Perry's apprentice he would be difficult to catch, but it wasn't her job to catch him, so she'd simply occupy her spare time with a hunch that could potentially catch a serial killer, or lead to a huge waste of time. Either way, she was using time she didn't need or want anyhow.

~

A few days later the phone rang in the middle of the night pulling Rian out of the middle of a dream with Ari wrapped tightly in her arms. She opened her eyes in the darkness and tossed the pillow she was clutching to the floor in disgust.

"Casey."

"Rian, Captain Burke here, I want you to head out to Kerns. There's a homicide call and I want you to see if this is similar to your hunch. Let me know what you find out." He hung up before she could reply.

Rian dressed quickly and hurried across town. She wasn't thrilled about seeing a dead body. During her short time working with cold cases she'd seen more dead body pictures than she could count and her mind always seemed to find a way to twist the picture into Ari's dead body on the sidewalk.

When she arrived on scene there were two other detectives that weren't at all thrilled to see her at their crime scene and the medical examiner, a slightly shorter woman with long dark hair pulled back in a ponytail and light brown eyes that seemed to growl every time Rian got close to the body.

"Casey you're here to observe and that's all," one of the detectives said as he spit tobacco into a paper coffee cup. Rian nodded and pulled a small notebook from her inside jacket pocket.

The victim was a middle-aged white male with a large caliber gunshot wound. Rian made notes of the scene and all of the buildings in both directions as far as she could see in the dark. When the medical examiner rolled him to the side Rian noticed most of the left portion of the back of his skull was missing.

"Exit wound," Rian said to herself.

"Yes, Sherlock, that would be were the bullet exited and took half of his head with it," the medical examiner said sarcastically.

"I actually wasn't talking to you," Rian said as she moved around to the other side of the road to make a few more notes about the scene.

"Who invited her?" The medical examiner asked the detective with the coffee cup as she nodded in Rian's direction.

"I sure as hell didn't. The captain said she has a hunch or some shit about a cold case. As far as I'm concerned she couldn't find her way out of a paper bag, much less solve a homicide case. But, hey I'm not some washed up retired federal agent now am I?" he said and spit into the cup again.

Rian walked back over to the body. "Any idea on the caliber or distance?" she asked the medical examiner. That's when she noticed the name on her I.D. badge was Leann Swanson.

"Nope. I'm not a fancy big time agent, I have to go back to my lab to figure out the specifics, but maybe you can enlighten us," she said.

Rian looked at the two of them and walked away. She was halfway to her unmarked car when she turned back around. "If the two of you were even half as competent as a *washed up retired federal agent* you would know it was a .308 caliber and shot from at least two hundred yards away," she calmly said before walking away.

When Rian got in her car she let her frustration roll of her back and dialed the Captain's number. He was surprised to hear all of the information that she'd given him, but he didn't see a need to scour the rooftops for spent cartridges. He denied her request and sent her back to her cold case assignment, which, was fine with her. She expressed her desire to stay away from homicide when she was hired. She had no desire to work active cases and she didn't have the drive to pursue suspects on a high priority level. The fire that drove that ambition in her went out a long time ago.

The next afternoon the phone rang in the cold case room. Rian yawned and answered it. She was tired from being up in the middle of the night and was too awake to go back to sleep once she got back to her tiny apartment.

"This is Leann, the medical examiner from last night,"

"I know who you are," Rian cut her off.

"Well, I need you to come down to my office within the hour."

Rian checked her watch, it was nearing her lunch hour and she really didn't want to spend it in the M.E.'s office with a dead body. "I'm about to go to lunch."

"My office is in building C, third floor," she said just before the line went dead.

"I know where it is," Rian said to herself.

~

Rian walked into the M.E.'s office close to two hours later with a fast food cup in her hand. She took a sip from the straw causing it to slurp. Leann turned around, the sharp crease in her brow said it all, she was pissed. Rian walked further into the room.

"It's about time you showed up," Leann spat and snatched the sheet off the gunshot victim's body. He was gray in color and naked. He looked peaceful until you noticed the small hole on one side of his head and the other side of his skull missing. Rian visibly flinched and backed away slightly.

"I told you I was going to lunch. I'm not even sure why you called me down here, I work cold cases."

"You knew things, at the crime scene, details no one else knew," Leann said with a little too much accusation in her voice.

Rian shrugged she wasn't in the mood to give a mathematical lesson, caliber patterns was basic geometry 101. She'd learned the simple formulas and detection methods during her first year at the academy. She slurped her drink again.

"How did you know the details?"

"Call it intuition," Rian simply stated.

"Sounds more like suspicion to me."

Rian slurped the last of her drink and tossed it in the trash can. "There's your DNA sample let me know if it matches anything you found at that clean crime scene. Otherwise, stop wasting my time with useless bullshit. I was a federal agent. I don't need to justify my knowledge or training to you or anyone else in this goddamn building. Now, if you or the detectives on this case would like to know my theory or how I came up with it I will gladly explain it to you," she said and walked out the door.

As soon as Rian was back at her desk her cell phone rang. The captain called her into his office. She had a feeling this would happen so she grabbed the file she was working on and went down to his office a few floors below her.

"Care to explain," he said when she sat down.

"There isn't anything to explain. You asked me to go observe a crime scene, I did that. Your medical examiner decided to question me like a suspect so I left."

"I see. I am a little curious as to how you knew the details myself. I know federal agents are trained at a higher level than us city folk, but you were perfectly accurate and I've never heard of that before," he said and leaned back in his squeaky chair.

Rian bit back the sarcastic response she wanted to give. "Captain, I explained that this cold case I ran across had similarities to the federal case I had worked. Based on the information from both cases I came up with a hypothesis, which I briefed you on. At that crime scene I simply took in the surroundings and lack of evidence. When I visually examined the body the entrance and exit wounds were obvious based on my high level training, as you put it. I was able to come to the conclusion that the victim was shot with a long range high-powered rifle. Based on the entrance hole the caliber looked like a .308, and the exit wound and perceived bullet path led me to think it was at a long range of at least a hundred yards. I explained most of this on the phone last night, which was why I wanted to take a look at a few rooftops in that range."

"All right, if you come up with anything else get it to the detectives on the case without hesitation. I also want you to take that cold case information to Leann and work with her to see if we can put some proof behind any of these similarities. We work together in this department

Casey." He chewed the side of his lip and waited for a response, when she didn't give one he dismissed her.

Rian spent the rest of her day buried in cold case files. She had all of the shootings for the past four years separated into multiple piles. There were no other random shootings in their jurisdiction but she was willing to bet there were others in the state.

The next morning she called the M.E.'s office and got Leann's voicemail. She left a brief message to have her call returned and left her cell number. She decided to make a few calls to other large cities in the state to see if any of them had unsolved random shooting cases from the past four or five years. None of the other departments could give her specifics, but they all said they'd do some research and call her back. She wondered if anyone would actually follow up. If she flashed her federal badge they'd surely jump through hoops to get her the information she was requesting. She missed the high priority that came with the title, but she didn't miss the high profile cases.

It was ironic how she was working on a random shooting case when a random drive by shooting was how Ari was murdered. She wondered if there were any leads. It had been a few months since she resigned and she hadn't heard from anyone, so more than likely the trail went cold. Ari's murder would probably remain unsolved. This made her think about her case against the Argentine crime boss Fiorino Canturri. The case she worked on for two long years and hundreds of hours. She hadn't heard of anything in the national news, so it was probably collecting dust too. She wondered what happened to it and who it had been assigned to. She was so close to finally being able to nail that bastard, and then her whole life was turned upside down.

Chapter Seven

An hour later, Rian's thoughts were brought back to reality when her cell phone rang.

"Casey," she said without looking at the caller ID.

"It's Leann, I got your message. What's this about?"

"The captain says we need to play nice and I need to share my file with you," Rian sounded like a scolded child.

"Is that so," Leann laughed.

"When and where do you want to meet?" Rian said sarcastically ignoring the laughter.

"How long is this going to take?"

"I don't fucking know. I have a cold case and some information on an old federal case that are both similar to this latest homicide and I need to see if they all jive. So, it can be ten minutes or two hours. Just tell me when and where so I can get this over with."

Leann rolled her eyes at the phone and opened her schedule book. "I'm tied up for the rest of the afternoon. Can you meet me this evening?"

"That's fine. Where?"

"How about your place?" Leann said.

"Not going to happen," Rian said flatly.

"I have a roommate so my house is out. What about your office?"

"It's more like a file room with a rickety piece of shit desk, but that's fine. Seven?"

"It's a date," Leann said sarcastically and hung up.

~

Rian and Leann put all of the information from the two files they had together and Rian looked up as much information on Jacob Perry as she could access since she was no longer a member of the bureau. They ordered Chinese food after two hours and were still working over an hour later.

"I wish I had autopsied this woman," Leann said as she flipped through the cold case file. "I was moved to this district later that same year. I did work with him though. Melvin Pierson was thorough, but old and came to his conclusions a little too easily. He retired at the beginning of the following year."

"Was he in someone's pocket?" Rian asked.

"Oh no. I don't know, he just didn't take the time to really cross the T's and dot the I's. It annoyed the hell out of me, but I was new to the district so I just went along with it."

"He didn't put any measurements in his file. There's no bullet caliber, not even a guess, and there aren't any suspected heights or distances for the bullet path. According to his chart she was simply shot with a high-powered rifle and it wasn't close range. That leaves an open book so large it would take two lifetimes to go through all of the possibilities," Rian said in frustration.

"You said Jacob Perry used tactical hunting rifles, right?"

"Yeah, mostly .270 and .30-06 and he was always three hundred to six hundred yards away. He had military sharp shooting training."

"How did you catch him?" Leann asked curiously.

"I wasn't involved. The case was sort of like a training case that multiple agents worked on. I was based in Chicago and in the span of two years he killed a dozen random people. He left no one alive, always a shot through the head. One night I got a call that he had been identified and apprehended. By that time, I was working on other cases and had moved on. A year later, I was assigned to D.C. I heard he was executed. I checked the database and it looks like it was close to four years ago. That's why I went back four years. If this is his apprentice then he's been killing randomly for about four years."

"What made you leave the FBI?"

Rian didn't answer, instead she opened the case folder for the most recent homicide.

"You don't talk much do you?" Leanne said.

"We're talking about these cases aren't we?" Rian said sarcastically.

"You really are as cold as everyone says you are."

"Look, I don't care what anyone says about me. My personal life is just that, *personal*. I retired, period. Now, if you have questions about these cases I will talk all you want."

"Fine, since you seem to know calibers and all of that fancy stuff, what do you think the numbers are with your cold case victim?"

"The pictures are inconclusive. Entrance wound looks like a .308 maybe a .270. I don't know. The back of her head is completely gone so it's definitely a hunting rifle. The bullets have large grain weights and are made to open into a huge pattern," She opened her hands to demonstrate. "It's called a dead kill. If a hunter shoots an animal they want it to drop right in that spot, die instantly. Otherwise, they may never find it. That's why the bullets open and make a huge path. Regular bullets with a smaller grain weight are made to be more of a through and through path. Without seeing the holes personally I can't give you an accurate number. The shooter was definitely long distance, but I don't think a hundred yards."

"What makes you think that?"

"Well," Rian took a blank piece of paper and a pen and drew a sideways cone shape that covered most of the paper. "See, these are the sizes of the exit hole. You read it backwards like this," she turned it around and wrote some numbers. "This is bullet speed based in yards. So, if you take a bullet, say shot from a hundred yards then you are looking at this size hole based on the speed because of the distance. Now, if you speed the bullet up by shooting it from a shorter distance say fifty yards the bullet is traveling much faster and hits the target sooner causing a larger hole. So hunters that are hunting from a long distance or sharp shooters that shoot up to a mile in distance use certain grain weights to compensate so the hole is still large enough for the dead kill."

"Wow," Leann was impressed. "Are you a hunter or did you learn this in the FBI academy?"

Rian smiled thinly. "The academy teaches you things you never thought you'd need to know. Algebra is used but geometry is major, it's used a lot in determining facts."

"So, based on your theory and your drawing, the cold case victim was shot from a shorter distance than our guy the other night. Correct?"

"Yes. She was also shot from a much shorter distance than Jacob Perry shot from. So, if this is his apprentice I have a feeling this woman could have been his first victim. He shot her from a shorter distance of around fifty yards to make sure he got the kill shot and it was a dead kill. He's getting better because our guy the other night was around two hundred yards. He's progressing and he's been doing this for at least four years, so there are others more than likely all over the state. Perry's victims were all over Illinois, at least six or eight cities I think."

"Why isn't the captain working on getting other cold case files that match this profile?" she said.

"He wanted us to meet first to see if you agreed with me I guess. I don't know. It's not my problem, I don't work homicide."

"Why don't you?"

"Don't want to."

"You're obviously good at what you do Rian. You're wasting your talent and skills working cold cases."

Rian shrugged. "It's my talent, skills, and life to waste, not yours."

Leann stared at her for a minute and quietly closed all of the files. "I'll get with the captain in the morning and let him know what we came up with."

~

Rian poured a ice filled glass of whiskey when she walked inside her tiny one bedroom apartment. The walls were dark and bare and the place was scarcely furnished. A shabby brown couch sat along one wall and a TV was across from it on a small stand. She sat on the couch and kicked her shoes off. The first sip was always the hardest, once she was past it the rest were swallowed easily.

Chapter Eight

"Hey Leann I heard you and the Ice Bitch worked on my case last night," the detective said as he spit into the paper cup.

Leann looked up from the autopsy she was doing and rolled her eyes. "Yes, Carl, I worked with Detective Casey last night. The captain asked us to put a few cases together and see if we could find some forensic similarities."

"How did that go?"

"She's actually very smart. I think we may have a serial killer on our hands. If I'm right you will want her on your side," she said. She made some notes on her file for the current body on the slab next to her.

"She's a hot-headed federal agent that has the personality of a wet mop. I'm not wasting my time with her. You can befriend her all you want, just give me the info you have for my case," he spit in the cup again.

"The captain didn't give it you?"

"No, he said to see you."

"Uh huh, are you sure he didn't say see Casey?"

"I don't give a shit, you were with her I'm sure you have the same info."

"Carl, have you ever wondered why she's the way she is? I mean who retires from the FBI while they're in their thirties with so many years ahead of them?"

"I don't care. She pissed away her career that's not my problem."

She shook her head. "I didn't want to work with her either after the way she's treated everyone around here, but she's not as bad as you guys make her out to be. Maybe it's because she's smarter than all of you put together," She slammed her desk drawer open and handed him a small notepad. "Everything's in there."

"She's a dyke you know. I'd watch out if I were you," he said on his way out.

"And you're a dick so what," she said to the empty room.

~

Rian walked into the M.E.'s office after lunch with two cups of coffee in her hand. She set one in front of Leann and took a sip from the other. "I figured you'd need this if you're as tired as I am."

"Thanks." Leann smiled.

"Have you talked to the captain today?" Rian asked.

"No, why? Carl Quinn was in here this morning giving me the third degree. I'm assuming the captain's making him follow your lead." She took a long swallow of the hot coffee. Her body thanked her.

"Oh really, I haven't heard about that. I'm sure he's pissed. He thinks I'm as dumb as a soup sandwich," she smiled thinly. Nothing could make her fully smile the way she used to.

"Boy does he have a rude awakening coming then," she laughed.

Rian shrugged. "Not my problem, anyway I came over here to see if you knew they were exhuming Monica Hillenbrand's body this week."

"You're shitting me." She took another sip and set the cup down. "How did they get a warrant for that?"

"I guess the captain called the family and told them we may have a new lead and need to check for additional evidence that may have gone unnoticed then because of technology or some shit. Anyway, the family agreed to it."

Before Leann could say anything her office phone rang. She answered quickly and after a minute she hung up. "Looks like I have to be at Sacred Heart Cemetery Thursday at eight a.m."

"I'm going too. Until there is definite proof these shootings are the same person I am still on the case because it's technically a cold case," Rian said.

"What happens when everything falls into place? Are you going to work the active case?"

"I don't work homicide," Rian said coldly.

"Don't you want to be involved? I mean if this is really the same person you are the reason we are this much closer to solving the case."

"The captain has called in favors to multiple cities asking to speed up the cold case file search that I asked for a few days ago. So, I'll have my hands full matching other cases to our profile if we get any other random victims. Which, I have a strong feeling we will."

~

Three days later, Rian was standing in the same spot with a surgical mask over her mouth and nose to help quell the stench of the dead as she examined the entrance and exit wounds on Monica Hillenbrand's head.

"Definitely a .308," she said as she made some notes on her notepad she kept in her jacket pocket.

"I agree, it measures almost exactly the same as Oscar Woodburn, our current victim. Do you still think the range is shorter?" Leann asked.

"Absolutely. Our shooter was no more than fifty yards away. I'm going to go ahead and say I'm almost positive she was the first victim. He was nervous, almost missed his mark. That's why the shot is so high above her forehead and into her hairline."

"Did you work as a profiler in the FBI?" Leann watched Rian's body involuntarily move away when she mentioned the FBI.

"No."

"You seem to know so much, that's why I asked."

"It's all part of the training. Unless, you work internet crimes or something like that, otherwise you go through homicide training and profiling."

"So, you worked in high-profile homicide cases then?"

"No." Rian said without looking at her.

"Okay?"

"Leann, obviously you haven't caught on to the fact that I don't talk about the FBI or my involvement with the bureau."

"I understand that, Rian. I was just asking what kind of cases you worked," she said with a shake of her head.

"Organized crime," Rian almost whispered.

Leann looked up at her. Rian's skin was pale and she looked like she was lost in thought. She wanted to ask a hundred questions, but decided to move on and let Rian fight her ghosts on her own.

"So, the captain has three other random shooting cases that are being sent to us. I should have them by this evening," Rian said.

"Looks like another long night," Leann grinned.

"You don't have to work them with me if you don't want to. It'll probably take all night."

"I'm sure the captain will call and order me to anyway, so it's not a problem. We should really find somewhere else to work besides that tiny little office of yours and mine smells like formaldehyde at the moment."

Rian swallowed the lump in her throat. "My apartment isn't much bigger and it probably smells too, but I guess we can meet there. I'll text you the address when I get the files."

"Okay, I'll pick up a pizza and beer or something," Leann said as Rian nodded and left the room.

Rian sat at the rickety desk she called her own and stared at the ceiling. She knew there was nothing wrong with working with Leann at her apartment, but she still felt weird about having someone else in her private space.

Maybe working with Leann was a good thing. She needed some kind of humanity in her life. All she'd been doing for the past three months was working and drinking herself to sleep most nights. She never went anywhere. Her meals were all take out or drive thru. She'd even lost weight from eating unhealthy. She needed to move on, she just didn't know how.

~

Leann wasn't shocked when she walked into the tiny apartment. She barely knew Rian Casey, but she expected the apartment to be cold and empty like the shell of a person that lived there. She wished she knew what Rian's story was. In some ways, the reclusive detective intrigued her. There was a story there somewhere buried deep inside Rian. She'd researched as far as she could and barely scratched the surface on Rian's life before she moved to Portland. Leann pictured her as a vibrant, thriving woman that took the lead and never followed.

"Thanks for bringing dinner. I was starving," Rian said. They'd been working for three and a half hours on the new cases.

"You're welcome. From the looks of your kitchen you don't have many meals here, or they are all take out."

Rian nodded. "Something like that."

Leann flipped her notepad to a new page. "What do you think about this victim in Eugene?"

"The same thing I think about all three of them. They are too random to be connected, yet they are similar in a number of ways. I think he's been working the state for at least three years and with every victim he gets a little better, a little cleaner."

"Two of them are .30-06 caliber and not .308. Why do you think that is?" Leanne asked.

"Easy, he was either trying a new caliber on his own terms, or he did it to keep the authorities guessing. As long as these shootings keep getting reported as random acts of violence he knows he's getting away with it. It's a game. He shoots someone and watches the news to see how it's handled. After a number of months, I think he just decides it's been enough time and he goes somewhere else and does it again. We have five cases that span over three years. My guess is he's hitting two a year. Not enough to cause a flag, but enough to keep himself satisfied with the hunt." Rian didn't notice Leann staring at her.

"Why do you think he chose Oregon? Wasn't Illinois the state Perry worked in?"

Rian shrugged. "Could be any number of reasons. Maybe he's from here. Maybe he did a report on this state in second grade." She almost cracked a smile but hesitated when she looked up into brown eyes staring at her from a few feet away. She knew that look and the burning sensation deep down that came with it. Rian cleared her throat and focused her eyes on the files spread across the table in front of her.

"Did the FBI teach you how to read people too?" Leanne said when Rian purposefully looked away from her.

"You'd be surprised at what the FBI taught me. Most of its classified and can never be disclosed." Rian's voice sounded hollow. It frustrated Leann to see some light trying to break through only to be extinguished before it reached the surface.

"How long have you been retired?"

"Maybe we should call it a night. I think we've got everything we need here. I'll get it to the captain in the morning," Rian said as she stood up and stretched her sore back. She was getting too thin, the belt around her waist was holding on to her hipbones for dear life.

Leann walked towards the door, but stopped short of opening it. "Rian, I can't make it go away, whatever darkness you have haunting you, but I'm here if you ever want to talk about it."

Rian watched her leave and wiped the lone tear that was threatening to fall. Every time she thought about the FBI she thought about Ari. Leann's obsessive curiosity was driving the darkness that Rian was trying so hard to let go of.

Chapter Nine

Rian was surprised when her phone rang with a Washington D.C. area code. She almost didn't answer it. Section Chief Walsh was in town and wanted to meet for lunch. She wanted to say no, but she named a time and place and showed up willingly. After the morning she'd had dealing with the captain and Carl Quinn she actually looking forward to seeing a familiar, friendly face.

"How's life on the other side of the country?" Philip Walsh asked when he sat down in front of Rian.

"Its life, I guess," she said. "Why are you here?"

"I can't come check on my best agent and see how you're doing?"

"I'm not an agent anymore," her voice faded to a whisper.

"Once an agent, always an agent," he said firmly as he slid a file across the table.

"What's this?"

"New development on Fiorino Canturri. I thought you might want to see it."

She slid the file back. "I'm not interested in Canturri, not anymore."

"This may change your mind."

"Damn it, Walsh, I'm not in the bureau anymore. I don't care what's in that file or what the latest news is. If you catch him I'll see it in the news. I'm trying to move on with my life. I don't need this right now." She stood to leave and he opened the file and slid it towards her. She jerked back so hard she knocked her chair to the floor. Ari's beautiful face was staring back her.

"Is this some kind of sick joke? You bastard," she yelled.

"Sit down, Rian!" he said firmly. "The woman in that picture is Arianna Canturri, Fiorino Canturri's daughter."

Rian shook her head no. She closed the file and pushed it away. Her blood was boiling. How dare he come to her with some crazy claim. If Ari was related to that cold-hearted son-of-a-bitch she'd know it. She worked day and night on his case for two years. She practically knew when the man took a shit. There was no way he had a daughter, and it definitely wasn't the same woman she was planning to spend the rest of her life with and watched die slowly in her arms.

"Arianna Canturri left Argentina. Well from the reports I'm getting she ran away from her father sometime before she met you. Apparently, she fled to the States and hid away in a coffee shop using the alias Ari Turner."

Rian picked the chair up and sat down. "There's no way, Walsh. She knew I worked in organized crime. She knew I traveled to Argentina and Brazil. If that's true why would she be with me?" Rian hung her head in her hands.

"I don't know. Maybe she was working for him. I know you kept your files and laptop with you all the time. Do you think she ever got into it?"

"Don't go there Walsh," she growled. "My Ari was sweet and innocent. She wasn't working for that monster. There is no way it's the same girl."

"When I got the information from the crime scene after she died I noticed a few discrepancies so I dug around. Ari's finger prints led me to a match in International Crimes. I sent a DNA sample and it matched as well. Your Ari was Fiorino Canturri's daughter. I'm sorry."

"She wasn't working for him. I'd bet my life on it. No way," Rian said as she stared out the window.

"Somehow he found her and that may have led him to you."

"Are you saying he killed her because of me?"

"If she wasn't working for him and he found out she was lying down with a federal agent, yeah he probably thought she had become a threat."

Rian wiped the tear that rolled down her face. "Why are you telling me this? Why now? She's been dead for six months."

"I need to know if there is anything you may have told her, or that she may have found. We have to stop him."

"You came here and turned my life upside down and all you can say is do I have anything that will help your case," Rian shook her head. "I knew you were heartless, but this is low even for you, Walsh."

"I did everything I could to help you from the moment I got the call," Walsh gritted his teeth.

"All you care about is that damn agency. Well, that agency can go to hell," Rian stood up. "You have everything I ever had on Canturri and his organization. As far as I'm concerned the information you brought here should never have been disclosed to me." She walked a few feet and turned around. "You should never have told me, Walsh."

~

After a handful of glasses of whiskey Rian dried the tears from her face and opened the locked file box she kept under her bed. She spread the pages around the dining room table and began sifting through the case that ran her life and potentially killed the only person she'd ever loved. A person that may have double-crossed her. A person that lost her life because of her.

Rian had learned a few months before Ari's death that Canturri had a daughter with a maid that was killed after she tried to flee with the child. Rian had no idea how old the child was or her name. He also had a son named Valentino that was working as one of his second hands and learning the business. Rian assumed since there was no trace of the daughter that she possibly died when the mother died.

Rian stared at the piles of papers and pictures littering the table. She couldn't understand how someone could kill their own child. She picked up the satellite picture of Fiorino Canturri walking out of his compound.

"I'll kill you myself if I find out you did this to her because of me," she said as she silently vowed to continue her work on his case. It was her job to bring him down and he took the most important thing in her life away from her. She wouldn't stop until he was where he belonged, whether it was behind bars or six foot under the dirt didn't matter to her anymore.

Chapter Ten

Captain Burke flipped a page in the folder he was holding as he rocked in his squeaky chair. Rian made a mental note to sneak in there with some spray grease. The squeaking was like nails on a chalk board to her. She watched him pick his teeth and rub his hand across the scruff of five o'clock shadow that was already starting.

"You make some good points here, Casey, but I just don't know. It's similar enough to be the same person but so random and vague that the theory you have here seems pretty farfetched. If I were a gambling man," he put the folder down and looked at her, "I'd go with my gut here, and my gut's telling me there's a chance it could be the same person, but I don't see any link to Jacob Perry. He's dead and gone anyway, so that doesn't really matter. This is what I'm going to do, I want you to work with Quinn on this and see if you can come up with a pattern to follow."

"Captain, with all due respect, I work cold cases. Shouldn't Quinn be working this case with someone else since it's active?"

"At the moment, the case is cold anyway. Besides, you seem to know a lot about the cases and if your theory is right Quinn will need your knowledge. Most detectives would jump on the opportunity to work an active case and a potential serial killer at that."

"I understand that, but I'm not most detectives, Sir."

"Why are you here, Casey?"

"What do you mean?"

"I told myself it was none of my business, but I have to ask. Why did you leave the FBI to work in a tiny stale room shuffling cold cases?"

Rian took a deep breath. "I didn't belong there anymore."

"I see."

"Captain, I took the job working cold cases because I don't want to work active cases. I don't care to be called to a crime scene in the middle of the night, or burning the midnight oil trying to catch a suspect."

"What *do* you want, Detective Casey?"

"If I can help potentially solve a crime and put away a criminal, that's great. That means I did my job, and my job here is to read old cases and try to find new leads. New leads for the active case detectives to handle, not me. That's what I want to do, Sir, the job I was given when you hired me."

"I can't say I understand, but there is no way of knowing what you did or saw working as a government agent that made you want to hide away like you do. I do know you're very good at what you do. No one can compare to the knowledge and training you have, so I hired you with the expectation that I could have you put those skills to use when I needed them. I don't care if you hide in cold cases for the rest of your life, but right now I need those skills. You proved to me this could be a serial killer and a very serious case and your help is needed until we either catch him or prove you wrong."

Rian nodded.

"You don't have to actively work the case. Quinn can come to you when he gets information and you can work together with Dr. Swanson. No one knows how to make a dead body talk like Leann does. Besides, like you said it's pretty much a waiting game until he strikes again."

~

"If I didn't know better I'd say you were hiding from me," Leann smiled when she walked into Rian's tiny office. Her rickety metal desk was surrounded by file boxes and you could barely see her in the middle.

"I'm not a fan of dead bodies," Rian said without looking up from the file she was reading.

"Uh huh," Leann laughed and set a cup of coffee in front of her.

"What's this for?" Rian said taking a sip.

"Friendly gesture I guess. So, do you have anything new on our case?"

"Nope, not since you asked me two weeks ago. Quinn's doing all of the leg work, if he's even doing it I have no idea. It's not my case and not my problem."

"What's got you all grumpy again? I thought we were getting past all of that?" Leann looked for a place to sit but decided to get out of the doorway and lean against the desk instead.

Rian looked up at her, but didn't say anything.

"What?" Leann asked.

"I'm sorry, I know you're trying to befriend me and I'm not really the befriending type. Not anymore anyway. I've had a lot on my plate lately and the captain is like a cat licking his balls. His management skills are severely lacking and I don't think he even cares anymore. So, I'm sure Quinn's probably not pursuing anything I gave him, which means the case is growing colder by the day."

Leann laughed. "I don't think I want to picture the captain with his leg over his head licking his balls. Anyway, you're right. Quinn can't stand you so I doubt he's even working the case at all. It'll come back on them when another body turns up."

"No, it'll come back on you and me because we'll have to do all of the leg work again while those two drag their feet," Rian stated.

"Why do you stay here? Someone with your talent could be doing anything. Instead, you chose to sit in a musty room reading old papers and looking at crime scene photos all day and doing the homicide detectives' dirty work. I don't understand it."

Rian shrugged. "I don't think it's for anyone to understand. I'm here by choice, that's it."

"I suppose dead bodies could wait around forever, but I should probably get back to work. Don't disappear in here." Leann smiled, tossed her empty cup in the waste basket, and walked back down the hall. Rian stared at the empty doorway longer than she should have.

~

A week or so had passed since the day Leann brought Rian coffee in the middle of the day. She was surprised to see her on the other side of the peephole with take out on a Friday night. Rian wasn't expecting her, she wasn't expecting anyone and hadn't in a long time.

"What are you doing here?" Rian said when she opened the door.

"I'm sure you haven't eaten, so I picked up Mexican. I wanted to show you something I found when I went back over our notes," Leann said as she pushed past Rian and walked towards the kitchen table. She dropped the bag of food when she saw the papers and photos all over the table. "What's this?"

Rian picked the bag up and handed it to her and began putting everything into a neat pile. "It's nothing, just an old case."

"An old FBI case," Leann said enthusiastically.

"Yes, and therefore none of your business. Now, what is it you need to show me? And open that bag I'm starving," Rian said as she put the pile of papers and photos back into the box and disappeared down the hall with it.

~

An hour later, the takeout bag was empty and Rian was yawning. Leann was leaning back in her chair watching Rian.

"I don't know if you have anything here or not. Monica Hillenbrand's long lost son may be our guy, but we have nothing to go on. Steven Monahan hasn't used his name, social security number, or anything else in five years. Either way, I think you found us a lead," she said with a thin grin that could almost pass as a smile.

"I'll let you take this to Detective Quinn because he cares for you so much. I'm sure he will love to see you may have a suspect for him," Leann said.

Rian shook her head. "Quinn doesn't scare me. I do have better things to do than deal with his idiocies so I will meet with Captain Burke first thing in the morning and pass this on. I hope this guy is caught, but it's out of my hands now that they may have a lead."

"So, do these better things have anything to do with that FBI file you're hiding from me?" Leann watched Rian lean her head against the back of the chair. "You look like you've been burning the candle from both ends. It's barely ten and you're falling asleep."

Rian rolled her head towards Leann and yawned again. "I've been dealing with a personal matter that's causing me to sleep less I guess."

"That's a pretty vague answer." Leann raised an eyebrow.

"The FBI has this little thing called confidentiality and that means that file is off limits to you and your curious mind."

"Oh come on, I may have solved your case for you, the least you can do is show me a real FBI case."

Rian shook her head. "You haven't solved my case. Number one, it's not my case it's Detective Dick's, and two it's not solved until the suspect is either dead or behind bars."

"Well, I found the first and only suspect."

"Oh come on, you sound like a kid begging for a new toy," Rian said.

"Is this case the reason you're not an agent anymore?"

Rian stared at Leann for a moment and sighed, "Why are you so drawn to my past?"

"Maybe I'm just drawn to you," Leann said softly.

"Leann," Rian turned her head in the opposite direction. "Don't, this isn't a good time. There won't ever be a good time."

"Something broke you, Rian. I'm sorry if I want to know what it is. I can't help wanting to fix it."

"Why? Why would you want to get involved in something you know nothing about?"

"Because I get the feeling you're only a shell of the person you used to be and that bothers me. I've become friends with you these past few months and maybe I want to help."

Was Leann a friend? Rian was so tired of being tired she didn't know anything anymore. She didn't know how long the grieving period was, but after close to seven months she thought she'd be further along than she was. Special Agent Walsh's new information surely set her back a number of months. Going through that file was like pouring salt into an open wound over and over.

Rian stood up so fast it actually startled Leann and she backed away. Rian walked down the dark hallway without saying a word and returned with the locked file box.

"If you ever say anything to anyone about what is in this file you could become a threat and be killed with no questions asked. I told you I worked Organized Crime and this case is one of the highest profile cases the FBI has open. I was the senior agent on this case for two years before I retired...I was recently given some new information, that's what I've been working on late at night."

Leann sat up straight in her chair. "I understand. If you trust me enough to show this to me, than you trust me enough to know I'll take it to my grave."

Rian visible cringed and hesitated. "That's not unlikely," she said.

"What?" Leann said.

"Someone has already been killed over what's in this file. Someone who knew nothing about it," her voice was low and heavy. Rian flipped the file open and a picture of a balding man with hollow, light-brown eyes and a gray and white mustache and goatee slipped out. He was unaware of the camera, but seemed to be looking directly at it. Looking at his picture again for the thousand and some odd numbered time Rian still didn't see any resemblance.

"This is Fiorino Canturri. He's an Argentinean mob boss that runs guns and funds terrorist cells. I've been trying to get enough on him to have him extradited for over two years. He has a heavily guarded compound in Buenos Aires. This photo was taken from a satellite."

"Wow," Leann said as she looked at the picture.

Rian put the picture back and closed the file. "Seven months ago my fiancé was gunned down in a drive by while walking next to me on a sidewalk." Rian wiped the tear before it could fall. Leann watched the color drain from Rian's face and covered her mouth with her hand. She had no idea. She thought maybe Rian's working partner was killed or something, but not her lover.

"I'm so sorry, Rian."

Rian continued to stare at the closed file. "I found out a couple weeks ago that she was Canturri's daughter."

Leann gasped.

"I never knew. I mean I knew he had a daughter by a maid and he had the maid killed when she tried to run off with the kid. I never found out any other information on the kid. Apparently, she went to boarding school as a child and then a few years ago she ran off to the States. The woman I met looked nothing like him, didn't have an accent, and went by a slightly different name. I didn't even know his daughter's name until recently."

"Oh my god, Rian. That's crazy," Leann said.

"My fiancé and I were together for two years and she knew I was in the FBI, but she never once questioned my job. She wasn't interested. She loved life and wanted nothing to do with violence and crime. Her father had her killed because of me...I won't stop until I catch him or kill him, whatever comes first."

Leann sat in silence. The icy tone in Rian's voice sent chills up her spine. She couldn't imagine the hell this woman had been put through over the past months. She wondered how she survived it all mentally, especially these last few weeks.

"I don't expect you to understand, but maybe now you can see why I do things the way I do them," Rian said.

"Rian, I can't begin to tell you how sorry I am, and no you're right, I don't understand, who would? You're a stronger woman than I ever imagined." Leann waited for Rian to look her in the eyes. "I'm all in."

"What?" Rian raised an eyebrow.

"Whatever you're doing to catch him, I want to help. Whatever you need just let me know."

"Leann, you can't do that. This is an FBI investigation and I shouldn't even be involved anymore. The only reason I know the latest news is because my Special Agent In Charge came here to tell me as a personal courtesy. They don't know I have this copy of the file. I'm doing this all on my own."

"It doesn't have to be on your own."

"Yes it does. This conversation goes nowhere else. Don't bring it up at the department or anywhere else for that matter. Just forget what I told you tonight. It's for your own safety, Leann."

"Fine," Leann said. "When the time comes, I'll be here ready to help you."

Rian shook her head.

"Even Batman had a hard time accepting Robin's help, but look at them now. They're the dynamic duo," Leann teased. Rian shook away the grin on her face and locked the file box.

"What's your next move?"

"I thought I told you to forget everything," Rian said as she started down the hall with the box. When she returned Leann was standing by the front door.

"Easier said than done," she said as she shut the door behind her.

Chapter Eleven

It had been two weeks since Rian told the captain everything she and Leann found out about Steven Monahan, the missing son of the potential first victim. Captain Burke told her it was a long shot, but he made Carl Quinn pick up the lead to see where it would go with their limited resources. Rian wanted to slap the shit out both of them and bang their heads together to try and produce common sense. She often wondered why budget constraints were always the block in the road when it came to local and state police departments. If they wanted to solve crimes and put murderers behind bars, then cutting back their staff numbers or restricting investigations to certain monetary values was the wrong move to make.

She shrugged off her disappointment in the Portland P.D. and moved on to bigger and better things like booking a commercial flight to Buenos Aires. She told the captain she had a family matter to take care of back home and would be gone for a few days.

Rian was packing her bag when she heard the knock on her apartment door. She grabbed her gun from the nightstand and walked through the tiny space she still couldn't call home. Leann's distorted face was on the other side of the peephole. Rian tucked her gun into the back of her pants and pulled the door open.

"Can I help you?" she asked as Leann walked inside.

"That's what I came to ask you. I was in your building today and when I went looking for you I found out you'd taken a few personal days. What's up?"

"I have a personal thing to take care of. I'll be back in a few days," Rian stated nonchalantly.

"Where are you going?"

"Do you always have to ask me a hundred questions about everything? I should've never told you anything about my life. I'm starting to regret it."

"I know you're a very private person, Rian. I'm just trying to be a friend."

"I don't need friends."

Leann noticed Rian's passport sitting on the kitchen table next to a few papers. "Leaving the country?" she asked.

"Maybe."

"I'm coming with you."

"Leann," Rian sighed. "I don't have time for this. My flight is in a few hours and I have to be there early. This doesn't concern you."

"You're going to Argentina aren't you?"

Rian nodded.

"I can help you."

"I need to do this on my own. Please understand that. I'll call you when I get back in a few days. If you haven't heard from me in a week tell the landlord I passed away and pack my place up. Burn everything and forget you ever knew me."

"Rian, that's crazy!"

"Leann, just do it. You want to be a friend, well now is your chance. Come on, I really have to get moving before I miss my damn flight," she said as she shuffled her out the door.

~

Rian slept as much as she could on the eighteen hour flight. The rest of the time she studied the map to the Canturri compound. She hadn't really formed a plan. She was just going there to see if the man would even talk to her face to face. She had to know why he killed his own daughter. Maybe she was stupid for doing it this way. Maybe she was subconsciously planning her own death. Her life didn't matter to her anymore. She lived everyday only to see the day that bastard got everything he deserved.

When the plane was landing Rian couldn't believe how beautiful the scenery was. There were mountains everywhere with blue-green water in the background. She wondered how all of this beauty could mask such a horrible monster. She slipped easily through customs and rented an SUV the size of a Smart Car.

She drove straight to the hotel room she rented by the ocean in the coastal town Pinamar. She wondered if Ari had ever been to this stretch of beach. She wiped the tears away when she thought about her sitting in the brown sand watching the waves splash in the distance. Rian tossed her bag on the bed and changed into her bathing suit.

It was almost noon when she slipped under the salty waves. She stayed in the water swimming and floating until the sun moved two clicks, meaning two hours had passed based on the position it was in. As she got out of the water she wondered what heaven was like. Perhaps she had just experienced it in the blissful sun surrounded by warm ocean water.

She'd waited so long to stand face to face with the man in the pictures that always seemed to be looking back at her. It felt weird being so close to him and at the same time so close to a part of Ari she never knew. A deep dark part she had kept hidden.

~

The next morning, Rian drank a cup of coffee as the sun rose over the ocean. She was unarmed and plainly dressed in jeans and a polo shirt. She knew exactly where she was going since she had spent countless hours learning the roads all around the compound. The Argentinean Army base was over an hour away and close to the mountains. There was no other civilization near the compound for at least a five mile radius.

Rian drove the two and a half hour drive between her hotel and the compound in silence. She made sure to toss her cell phone in the ocean before she left just in case he killed her and traced her back to the hotel. His henchmen would find her suitcase with some clothes. She hid her passport in a loose brick in the parking garage of the airport when she circled back during the hours she spent riding around the coast. There would be no way to trace her to Leann or anyone else. She also made sure the locked file and other personal possessions were locked in a safe deposit box and in the event that she didn't return within a week the key to that box was set to be mailed anonymously to Leann in six months with instructions for her to secretly destroy it. She hoped she covered all of her tracks in case this unannounced meeting went horribly wrong.

When Rian pulled up to the entrance gate the guard pointed a gun in her face and asked who she was and what she wanted. Rian slowly handed him her Portland Driver's License. He opened her door and told her to get out with her hands on her head. She did as instructed. He patted her down.

"What are you doing here?" he said in broken English.

"I would like to talk to Fiorino Canturri face to face," she said.

The guard laughed, "Who do you think you are?" He pushed the gun into the back of her head. "Walk," he growled.

They walked the mile long road with Rian in the front with her hands on her head and his gun an inch from her hands. He talked on a cell phone in Spanish a few times, but kept walking right behind her. She was fluent in Spanish, but he was talking so low she could barely hear him. When they reached the double front doors two men in dark suits came out with guns drawn.

"What business do you have with Mr. Canturri?" One of the guys said as the other guy pat her down.

"It's in regards to his daughter, Arianna." she said.

"The American Agent came all this way to talk about Ms. Canturri," the man sneered and backhanded her across the face. Rian knew her lip split when she felt the blood run down her chin. It took everything she had to stand quietly on her feet and not shove that gun up his ass and pull the trigger.

When he hit her a second time she spit blood on the ground next to his boots. He hit her in the stomach forcing her to her knees.

She gasped and tried to stand back up but the guard held her arms behind her back. "I'm not an agent anymore. I'm alone. No one even knows I'm here," she said.

"That's enough," a deep voice said from inside the doorway. Rian looked to see Fiorino Canturri standing a few feet away. "You are very brave to come here American Agent."

"I do not work for the American Government anymore. I'm no longer an agent."

He snickered slightly and nodded his head. "Still, you come to my home."

"I want to know about Arianna," she said. The man in the suit smacked her across the face again, causing her to force herself to remain conscious.

"She is no longer a problem," he said with a laugh that disgusted Rian. She wanted to choke the life out of him with her bare hands.

"Why did you kill her?" she yelled.

"You worthless American. You come to my country, to my home, and question me." He spit on the ground directly in front of her. "You're not worth my time."

"You came to my country, into my life and took her from me. I want to know why," Rian said angrily. She flinched when the man in the suit swung his fist, connecting with the back of her head causing her to lurch forward. Rian could barely keep her eyes open, she was fading quickly.

Canturri laughed. "She's where she belongs now." He waved his hand to the men in the suits and walked away.

"Do you want us to kill her?"

Fiorino turned around and shrugged his shoulders. "Dump her in the ocean, alive."

"You heard him," he said to her. "Let's go."

~

Rian had no idea how long they had been riding in the speedboat. She was in and out of consciousness and she knew from experience that several of her ribs were cracked or broken. Taking a deep breath was absolutely impossible. Her face was so swollen she could barely see. When the speeding boat came to an abrupt stop she lurched forward slamming her head into the console causing everything to go black once again.

Rian's body sank slowly in the warm water. When the men were satisfied she was underwater long enough they sped away. The burning in Rian's lungs caused her to finally open her eyes. She was on her back surrounded by clear water. The sun was shining brightly above her as she sank lower and lower. The feeling was surreal. She wasn't sure if it was drowning or death or both. She could only find one reason to live, one reason to fight the excruciating pain in her lungs. Justice. If she lived through this she would make it her life's mission to bring Fiorino Canturri down.

Rian began kicking her legs and moving her arms, but the surface was coming fast enough. There was no breath to exhale to quell the burning from the water in her lungs. She was already lightheaded and dizzy from the multiple concussions she'd sustained and she was seconds away from passing out due to lack of oxygen. She breached the surface just as her body was about to give up. She coughed and struggled to breathe as the water came up. She laid there floating on the surface staring at the blue sky until she could breathe without coughing. Her body felt heavy. She was tired and in more physical pain than she'd ever felt in her life, but she righted herself and bobbed up and down with the current until she finally found the shoreline. She was a few miles away and there wasn't a boat in sight. She had no energy. There was nothing left, but she mustered up as much hatred as she could find. The adrenaline flowing through her veins gave her the strength to swim for her life despite the broken bones and bruises.

Rian swam and swam as the sun began to slowly sink below the horizon. She had no idea how long she was in the water or even where she was, but she finally hit the beach and collapsed.

Chapter Twelve

Rian awoke to a man and a woman checking her for a pulse. They were debating in Spanish what to do with her. The woman was saying CPR and when the man said *muerto*, dead Rian opened her eyes. The two people jumped back screaming as Rian began coughing.

"Are you okay?" the woman asked from a few feet away. "We will take you to the hospital."

"No. I'll be fine," Rian said. "Where am I?"

"Valeria del Mar," the man said.

Rian's head was pounding uncontrollably, her lungs were still burning, and the rest of her body just simply ached. She sat up and tried to get her bearings. She didn't have to check her pockets to know her rental car keys and wallet were missing. Thankfully, the only thing in her wallet was about two hundred and fifty Pesos or the equivalent of fifty U.S. Dollars. Her I.D. was hidden with her passport.

"What happened to you?" the woman asked.

"What day is it?" Rian asked.

"Friday," the man looked at his watch. "about eight a.m."

Rian tried to stand and the man quickly helped her to her feet. "Can we take you to the hospital?" he asked.

"No."

"You're American, yes?"

"Yes," Rian said.

"Are you hungry?" the woman stepped closer. Rian looked down at her. She couldn't remember the last time she'd eaten. She simply nodded.

"Come on, I will make you some soup," she said as she started walking up the beach. Rian didn't move.

"We live just up the beach that way." The man pointed. "It's safe."

Rian slowly followed. She needed to get some dry clothes and get to a phone. When they reached the small building it looked like a cluster of tiny apartments. The couple helped Rian inside and sat her at what appeared to be a kitchen table. She looked around at the eclectic decorations in the tiny room. The place was barely big enough to turn around in. She assumed the narrow hallway led to a bedroom and a bathroom.

"I will heat you a bowl of *cazuela,* vegetable soup." The woman poured the contents of a container from the refrigerator into a pot on the stove. The man made a cup of plain black coffee and set in front of her. Rian drank it in small sips while she waited for the soup to heat up. She kept one eye on the two people and the other eye on the door. She was somewhat familiar with Valeria del Mar. If she remembered correctly there were a few beachfront tourist shops down the street.

Rian was surprised at the flavors in the soup. It was mixture of vegetables with some sort of meat that she hoped wasn't rat or cat or some other inedible animal. Either way, she ate until the bowl was empty and didn't turn away when they offered a second bowl. When she felt enough strength coming back she used the restroom and thanked them, then headed towards the shopping district. She was thankful her face didn't look as bad as it felt. The saltwater must have helped with the swelling, but her lip was split in two places and there was obvious purple bruising on her cheeks and chin.

A few tourists looked at her and held their purses tight when she passed by them. Rian merely kept walking like she didn't notice. When she finally found the dimly lit store full of touristy clothes and gift items she retreated to the back with a t-shirt, shorts, and flip flops that looked like they would fit. She waded everything up in a ball and went out the backdoor without anyone noticing her. She walked as fast as her broken body would allow until she reached an alley blocked by dumpsters. She squeezed between them and quickly changed into the new items and tossed her wet, bloody clothes and shoes into one of the dumpsters and went back out on the street. In another store she snagged a pair of sunglasses.

She needed to find a way to the airport and without any pesos that was almost impossible. She was a couple hours from the airport where her stuff was stashed. She kept walking down the street like the rest of the tourists casually looking in cars to see if the keys were in the ignition.

At the tenth vehicle the keys were dangling in the ignition. It was some kind of delivery company, but that didn't matter. Rian jumped in, started the little car, and took off down the road shifting the gears as fast as she could. She wanted to laugh when she saw the gas gauge was below a quarter of a tank.

~

It didn't take Rian long to find how long the little car would go on a quarter of a tank. She was barely a half hour away when the fuel light started blinking. She pulled over at a small market and asked to use the phone.

When Leann answered Rian wanted to jump up and down. "Leann, it's Rian. I only have about thirty seconds, so listen close."

"Rian, oh my god, I was starting to get worried. Where are you?" Leann said. "Are you okay?"

"I had a small accident, but I'm fine. I'll be back sometime tomorrow. Listen, do you have a credit card handy?"

"What kind of accident?"

"Leann," Rian growled. "Credit card please."

Leann quickly ran the numbers off to the man on the other side of the counter. He ran the card for enough money to fill up the little car and when it went through he handed the phone back to Rian.

"Leann cut that card up and call and cancel it as soon as I hang up with you. I'll explain everything when I get back. I have to go," Rian hung up quickly and looked at the time on the wall clock. She'd been on the phone longer than she wanted. Rian nodded at the guy and filled up the little car.

When she reached the airport she left the car a few miles away and walked the rest of the distance. She was glad to see her small package was still tucked away neatly behind the loose brick. She grabbed her Oregon I.D. and passport and headed inside the airport.

~

The only return flight going in her direction had two layover stops which pushed the flight time over twenty hours. She wasn't happy, but at least she was on a plane and headed home. Once she arrived she called Leann to come pick her up since she'd taken a taxi to the airport to start with. She stood on the sidewalk in a yellow t-shirt that said *Doin' it Argentine Style*, a pair of hot pink cargo shorts, and blue flip flops that were slightly too small. Leann rode right past her and parked at the curb. Rian shook her head and walked towards the small gray car and knocked on the passenger window. Leann jerked back in the seat and cracked the window.

"Can I help you?"

"Leann, it's me. Open the damn door," Rian growled. When the lock popped she quickly got in and shut the door.

"What the hell happened to you?" Leann asked as she put the car in gear.

"Just drive."

"Where to? My house or yours?"

Rian thought about it for a minute. She doubted they were looking for her and more than likely thought she was dead. They probably didn't care either way. "Just go to mine," she said as she leaned back against the headrest.

Chapter Thirteen

It had been two weeks since Rian returned from Argentina. Leann didn't believe Rian's story of being in a car accident, so Rian finally told her she confronted Canturri and he politely let her know it was none of her business. She was lucky they didn't shoot her or dump her in the water with cement boots.

"Your bruises are almost healed," Leann said from the doorway. She stepped inside and handed Rian the cup of coffee she was holding. "How are your ribs?"

"Fine." Rian winced when she reached for the cup.

"Uh huh, I see that."

"Really, I'm fine, still a little tender, but I'll live."

"I just spoke with the captain. Quinn hasn't been able to track down Steven Monahan."

Rian shrugged. "I didn't think he was even looking for him. If Monahan's our guy he's hiding out somewhere. He may not even be in Oregon."

"What would you do if it was your case?"

"It's not."

"Humor me," Leann smiled.

Rian raised an eyebrow. "Since when does a medical examiner have so much interest in a case?"

"When it's a huge case that I may have solved," she smiled again. "Oh come on, I hack up dead people all day. Go easy on me. This case is exciting." She bit the corner of her lip and shrugged. "And you intrigue me."

"He's in Washington. California's too rich for him," Rian sipped her coffee. "He's not in Seattle either. Yakima feels more like home to him."

Leann shook her head. "You're too damn smart to be sitting at this desk reading cold cases. You're wasting your talents."

Rian stared at her. "I don't care anymore. I thought you might understand, I guess I was wrong."

"I wish you'd let me in. Let me help you."

"Leann,"

"Detective Casey, something came in the mail for you," a young guy said as he slipped past Leann and dropped a brown envelope on her desk.

"I'll bring over takeout later," Leann said as she left the room. Rian was too busy looking at the envelope to notice she'd left.

It was addressed to Rian Casey, Portland Police Department. There was nothing else on it. When she pulled the letter out it was some kind of code typed on old paper.

ZYHUMOQAWRXECPILSAGYOIBNVGRWQIJTGH
DFCIXRZE.DYHORUVNZEREWDQTLOFSKTBOYP
DBCEDFLOPRVEMYNODUHGKESTWBTUXRVNQ
EJD.KHAEVWZIDLFLIKSIELTLPYROGU.FHUEXD
LOWEASHNYORTVKXNMOQWAYGOHUZSFUWR

BVJITVPEGD.GCDOWNRSEIQDXESRHYBOYUFRD
SXEALNFMWPAZRKNLEID.
2.33744.37246336.2333.243438.886.

Rian read and reread the message, but nothing made sense to her. She slid the paper back into the envelope and put in her briefcase. She'd only seen a few ciphers while working with the FBI and knew she would need to figure out the key before she could decode the letter. That would take time and sitting at her work desk was not the best place.

~

Rian poured a glass of whiskey and sat down at the kitchen table in her apartment. The cipher letter was sitting in front of her. It had traces of black dust on it where Rian checked for finger prints. Whoever sent the letter wore gloves and there was no stamp to lick so she couldn't get DNA. She stared at the white paper full of numbers and letters that she was using as a scratch pad to try and figure out the key.

A loud knock on the door made her jump. She swallowed the last of the whiskey from the glass and grabbed her gun. She wasn't expecting anyone and after getting the mysterious delivery she was on her toes.

Leann's distorted face was staring back at her through the peephole in the door. Rian shook her head and tucked her gun under the couch cushion.

"What are you doing here?" she said when she pulled the door open. Leann was standing there with two steaming bags of something that smelled good. Rian's stomach growled.

"I said I was bringing takeout over. Didn't you hear me?" Leann said as she pushed past her and went to the table.

"No," Rian said to herself as she shut the door and followed her.

"What's this?" Leann said as she walked past the table. She set the bags on the kitchen counter and began separating the Italian dishes. "I got lasagna and spaghetti and meatballs with breadsticks. Which one do you want?"

"Spaghetti," Rian said.

"What's that on the table?"

Rian shook her head. Leann was getting too close and there was no way to stop her. "Confidentially?"

Leann turned around and raised an eyebrow. "Haven't I kept all of your secrets so far?"

"It's the delivery I got at the department today. It's a cipher."

Leann's eyes grew large. "You mean like a coded message?" The excitement in her voice was evident.

Rian sighed. "Yes, something like that."

"Who sent it?"

"I have no idea, but I'm sure it's connected to my recent trip."

Leann handed her a plate and sat next to her at the table. "What does it say?"

"I don't know yet," Rian said as she dug into the food in front of her. Eating didn't seem the same anymore and most times she forgot about it all together until her stomach reminded her.

"Do you think he sent it?" Leann said between bites.

Rian shook her head. "No. I think it's a warning of some kind." She quickly finished her food and set the plate to the side.

"I've only seen those in movies."

"Haven't you heard of the Zodiac?" Rian asked her.

"Well, yeah."

"He sent coded messages to the newspaper and the police and was never caught. I've seen a few of the originals. When I was in the academy one of the classes I had to take was about ciphers and codes. It was pretty basic unless you were going into cyber coding or another area of expertise. During one of the classes we got to see the Zodiac letters."

"Wow,"

"Many people have tried over the years to solve them, but no one has ever been able to come up with the codes for the last two," Rian said as she read her cipher again.

"The most interesting thing I saw in college were brains and body parts donated to science by family members of geniuses and famous people," Leann said.

Rian made a cringing face. "See, I think these numbers here on the bottom mean something. If I didn't know better I say it was the key."

"Why would someone give you the key with the code? Isn't the purpose of solving it finding out the key on your own?"

"Yes. Which is why I think it's someone trying to warn me. They want me to figure it out."

"Look at the first ten or so letters. If you take every other letter it's starting to spell something," Rian said as she started writing the separate letters on her scratch paper. "Maybe the two at the bottom means every second letter."

Leann starting following along. "But what about the rest of the numbers?"

"I don't know. Maybe the words in each sentence. You see these periods in the middle of the letters, those are probably end of sentences. Maybe these numbers are the letters in each word." Rian took the first block of numbers and wrote down every other letter until the period.

YOUAREPLAYINGWITHFIRE.

Rian blocked each word the way it should read and the number of the letters in each word matched the numbers on the bottom of the cipher. "I got it," she yelled as she began writing the rest of it out.

YOU ARE PLAYING WITH FIRE. YOU NEED TO STOP BEFORE YOU GET BURNED. HE WILL KILL YOU. HE DOES NOT KNOW YOU SURVIVED. CONSIDER YOURSELF WARNED.

Rian turned the paper to the side and showed it to Leann. She gasped when she read it.

"Who would send this to you?"

"I have no idea, but it's not going to stop me from getting that bastard."

"Who else knows you went there?"

"No one," Rian said. "There is satellite imaging that runs continuously. This could be from someone in the FBI that saw me in one of the images and recognized me. I honestly don't know."

"Wouldn't they just call you?"

Rian grinned thinly. "That would be too easy and traceable. If there is one thing the FBI teaches you it's how to be untraceable."

Leann nodded. "That's why you wanted me to destroy your stuff."

"Exactly."

"Are you ever going to tell me the whole story?" Leann said.

"Whole story about what?" Rian said as she put the letter and her scratch paper in the locked file box with the Canturri file.

"Your trip."

"There's nothing to tell. I went to the door, his henchmen bastards smacked me around. I borrowed some tourist clothes and came home." Rian said simply. "I need to pay you back for that gas I put on your credit card by the way."

"I'm not worried about thirty dollars," Leann said.

"I'm fine now, it's over. Fiorino Canturri will pay for everything he's done one day and when he does I'll be standing there watching from the sideline."

"I'm glad you're okay," Leann grabbed her hand. Rian squeezed her hand and pulled away.

"Leann,"

"I know," Leann said as she stood up. "Have you ever been to Kelley Point Park?"

"No. I know where it is though," Rian said. She'd stumbled on the historical park when she first moved to Portland and was driving around trying to learn the city. Walking around in the park and looking out at the water over the vista reminded her of Ari and she wasn't in the mood to bring that subject up, so she lied.

"If you take the paved path it winds toward the vista and there is a Lewis and Clark Statue on the right. Meet me at the benches there at noon, I'll bring lunch," Leann said.

"Why? Tomorrow's Saturday, maybe I want to sleep."

Leann laughed. "You barely sleep as it is. Come enjoy a picnic lunch with me in the park. The fresh air will help clear the cobwebs from your head. You've been cooped up in that old file room you call an office and this makeshift apartment for too long."

Rian stared at her.

"What do you want for lunch?"

"Why are you feeding me all of the time?" Rian asked.

"I'm scared you will starve to death if I don't," Leann teased.

"Fine. Noon. Turkey on wheat."

Chapter Fourteen

Rian wasn't happy about being in the park, but she did miss the fresh air and serenity she always felt surrounded by nature. It had been nine months since Ari died and she was slowly starting to breathe again. She watched a beautiful blue jay flying from tree to tree close by. The free spirited bird reminded her of Ari as it flew close by to check her out and then perched on a nearby tree to watch her from a distance. The crunch of gravel in the distance brought her back to reality.

"Hungry?" Leann walked over to the bench and sat down next to Rian. "I wondered if I was going to find this bench empty when I got here."

"You almost did," Rian paused. "I'm not a fan of parks, not anymore." she said softly.

"Did you go to the park a lot back home?" Leann said as she opened the bag she was carrying and handed Rian a sandwich.

"Something like that," Rian said.

"I love coming here. This is kind of like my thinking spot. It's the one place I can let my mind run free and clear and not have to worry about tissue samples, test results, and being called out to a crime scene in the middle of the night. I don't have to be associated with Portland P.D. during the hour or so I spend sitting here." Leann looked at Rian and smiled. "I'm glad I could share this with you."

Rian nodded. She understood completely. She loved going to the park and watching the river flow by with ducks and turtles swimming along with it while birds soared overhead. It was the most peaceful time in her life.

"I promise not to talk about work," Rian said. "But, the captain told me before I left yesterday that there's a new file being sent to us. Apparently, while I was gone there was a random shooting in Salem."

"Oh really, does it match our M.O.?"

"I don't know. He didn't have the details. He just said a woman was shot while standing at an ATM. There wasn't much to go on."

"When will we get the case?" Leann asked as she tossed her sandwich paper into the empty bag.

"I'm hoping Monday. If it looks like our guy I'm going to make some calls and see if I can get the details from Jacob Perry's file. That may help us I.D. him."

"Do you think Perry knew Steven Monahan?"

Rian shrugged. "It's possible. I'm going to try to find a connection if I can get the file." She finished her sandwich and put the wrapper in the bag.

"Any lead is better than nothing I guess." Leann leaned back and stretched her legs out in front of her. "What are you going to do about that letter you got?"

"Nothing. It's clean anyway. I don't scare easily and whoever sent it obviously knows I'm working the case again. If it's the FBI I'll get a personal visit next."

"That's nice of them." Leann laughed.

"Yeah." Rian shook her head. "I don't think they realize just how personal he's made this. I won't stop until he's behind bars or under the dirt and frankly the latter would be quite nice."

"Try not to get beat up again," Leann teased.

"War wounds," Rian said.

Leann rolled her eyes and sighed when her phone rang. She talked quickly and wrote down an address. "I'm on call all weekend and it looks like someone decided to check out early. I have to go to a possible suicide. What a lovely way to ruin my beautiful afternoon," she said sarcastically.

Rian grimaced. "Good luck with that."

"Thanks." Leann put her hand on Rian's and squeezed before she stood up. "I'll see you Monday. Call me when you get that file."

Rian watched her walk away and decided to stay a little longer and enjoy the natural serenity. It had been so long since she sat and listened to the trees and the wildlife.

~

Rian felt someone watching her, when she turned around there was no one there. She stared at the blue sky another minute or two, then walked over to the trash bin and tossed the bag in. She was about to walk away when she got the feeling again that someone was watching her, before she could turn and look she heard footsteps on the gravel.

"She loves you," a female voice said.

Rian's breath hitched in her chest. She knew that sweet innocent voice anywhere. She spun around to see a petite woman with long brown hair standing in front of her wearing an overcoat and dark sunglasses.

Confused, Rian stepped closer. "Who are you?" she asked the stranger.

The woman pulled her sunglasses off slowly revealing one green eye and one blue one. Rian jerked back and her chest constricted. "No," she said as she shook her head and backed away. "You died. I spread your ashes," she whispered. The woman a few feet away might have brown hair, but there was no mistaking those beautiful eyes that would give her away anywhere.

"I know, the service was beautiful," she said.

"You were there?" Rian's voice rose. She felt like she was looking at a ghost and her world was swirling out of control. She was confused, her head and chest were pounding in unison.

"I'm sorry, Rian."

"Why, Ari? Why?" Rian said.

"He found me and threatened to kill you if I didn't leave. It was the only way to save you," Ari said as a tear slipped down her cheek.

"Who are you?" Rian yelled. "I don't even know you. Is it Ari Turner or Arianna Canturri? Who was the woman I was in love with, the woman that shared my life?"

When Ari tried to answer Rian cut her off. "No, that woman died nine months ago. You can go back to wherever you came from." Rian turned to walk away she was so lost and confused. The pain of losing Ari didn't compare to the pain of knowing it was all fake and she was still alive.

"He's pissed and if you don't stop trying to take him down he will kill you, Rian. That's why I came to warn you."

"Consider me warned," Rian said as she walked away without looking back.

When she reached her vehicle, Rian called Section Chief Philip Walsh. When his voicemail picked up she told him she had something new on Canturri and if he wanted it he needed to be on a plane soon.

~

Monday morning Rian went through her normal routine in zombie mode. She barely spoke to anyone and was constantly watching for Ari to pop out from every corner. She was glad the file from Salem hadn't arrived. She didn't have the patience to work on the case right now with everything else that was going on. When Leann tried to make time to see her, Rian found reasons to be busy with something else.

Tuesday afternoon Walsh arrived and met her at the same coffee shop from last time. Rian was early. She kept her eyes on everyone in the room searching for the one person she didn't want to see ever again.

"You're not an agent anymore, Rian." Walsh said when he sat down. "I was trying to keep you out of this, but there are things you need to know," he opened a folder and pushed it over to her. "Ari's still alive. We've known for quite awhile now. I'm sorry I couldn't tell you."

"I know," Rian said. "She came to see me."

Rian watched the color drain from Walsh's face. "What...uh...what did she say?"

"She tried to warn me off Canturri," Rian said as she looked at the open file there were surveillance pictures of herself at Canturri's laying on the table.

"You're in too deep here, Rian."

"You should've told me Walsh, for the fact that we were once on the same team if nothing else." Rian said.

"I couldn't say anything. We've been working non-stop on this case since you left and we're closer than ever before. I couldn't jeopardize our new lead. I have an informant that has set up dealings with customs to bring in a container shipment full of military grade automatic weapons in a few weeks."

"Is she working for him?"

Walsh twisted in his seat. "I don't know, but if I had to guess I'd say yes. Probably all along, Rian. I'm sorry."

Rian listened to his story in silence as her mind raced. "I'll give you everything I have. It's going to take me a few days. I'll send it to you."

"That's fine. Let me know if you see her again or she leaves you any kind of contact information," he said as he stood up. "This will all be over soon."

Rian sat at the small table and drank her coffee while he walked away. The best part of her life was turning out to be one big joke. She wondered if Ari ever even loved her. She didn't know who or what to believe anymore. She took another sip of coffee when she realized she needed something a lot stronger. She tossed a few bills on the table and went home. No one at the department would notice if she didn't come back from lunch anyway.

~

The next morning Leann was sitting at Rian's desk when she walked in. Rian looked like something that crawled out from under the couch. Her short hair was messier than usual, her suit was slightly rumpled, and she was wearing dark sunglasses in the already dark building.

"You look like something the cat threw up," Leann said standing up. Rian walked around her and sat down.

"I feel like it too," Rian said as she opened the lid on her coffee and added more sugar from the packets she kept in her top drawer.

"What's going on?"

Rian took her sunglasses off, revealing large circles under her eyes from lack of sleep and everything else her body needed to keep going. She tossed a file on the desk. "The Salem homicide," she said.

"When did you get this?" Leann said as she opened it.

"Just now," Rian yawned.

"Then this isn't what's got you so run down," Leann said.

Rian stretched her sore muscles. She wasn't in the mood to tell anyone her dead fiancé was back in the flesh and her world had been turned upside because of it. Rian watched Leann flip through the file casually while waiting for her to explain. Leann was nothing if she wasn't persistent.

When Leann closed the file she looked up at Rian and raised an eyebrow.

"There's been a new development in that other case," Rian stated.

"What kind of development?"

 "A huge one."

"Really? This is good, right? I'm assuming you haven't slept in days. When's the last time you ate anything?" Leann said.

Rian shrugged. "I don't know." She had spent the last few days going over everything she had on Fiorino Canturri. She tried to put some faith behind Walsh's story about the informant and the container of drugs coming through customs, but it just didn't make sense. Canturri was smarter than that. This wasn't his normal mode of operation. She honestly wasn't sure when she slept or ate last.

"I'll bring some dinner over tonight. You can tell me all about it."

"That's not a good idea. In fact, it's probably best if you stay away from me for a while."

111

"What? That's crazy, Rian."

"Something big is about to happen and I have no idea what it is and I don't want you to be a part of it."

"Fine. What about the case here? We need to look at this new file and compare it to the others."

Leann was right. Rian had an actual job to do whether she wanted to do it or not. "I'm going to look at it today. I'll come see you if I find anything."

Leann left the room without looking back. She was upset, but Rian didn't know what else to do. She didn't want Leann involved in this mess swirling around her.

~

Leann was elbow deep in a body cavity when Rian walked in. She saw Rian enter the room and immediately go back outside. She shook her head and laughed. When she had the body covered and back in the freezer she peeled off the gown and gloves she was wearing and went to the door.

"You can come in now," she said when she popped her head out. Rian was leaning against the wall in the hallway.

"I have no idea how you do what you do," Rian said as she cringed. She still couldn't look at a dead body or blood without thinking of Ari and that only pissed her off.

"Someone has to do it," Leann grinned.

"I finished that file from Salem and I wanted to show it to you."

"Come in," Leann said as she held the door open for Rian. "Did you find something?"

Rian walked over to a side table and opened the file. "This woman, Pauline Whitten, was shot while taking money out of an ATM at a strip mall."

Leann looked at the pictures and the autopsy report. "He shot her in the back of the head. It looks like the bullet exited through her right eye with a downward trajectory."

"Yeah, he was up high and probably a couple hundred yards away," Rian said.

"The report only says, high-powered hunting rifle."

"I have a theory," Rian said. "ATM's usually have cameras, maybe it picked up something."

"The cameras that they have won't pick something up from that far away though."

"I know that. But, maybe it will show the path of the bullet before it struck her. We need to gather a few things and take a road trip."

"Did the captain tell you to do this? What about Quinn?" Leann asked.

"I think he has no confidence in Quinn. He said it's my theory so I have to go incase I'm wasting time and to take you with me because you have the equipment."

Leann smiled. "It has nothing to do with Quinn, you know. He's had you working this case from day one. He's just doing it on your terms so you don't think you're working an active case. He's utilizing your skills without your knowledge."

Rian closed the file and stared at Leann. "I never even thought of it that way. I guess I've been too wrapped up in my own pitiful mess to realize what was even going on here. This place isn't really work to me, it's more like something to pass the time," she shrugged.

An hour later they arrived at the crime scene. The machine had already been replaced. Rian stood in front of it and turned around. There were a number of buildings in the distance including another strip mall on the opposite side of the highway. The mall manager arrived shortly after with the disk that had the surveillance footage from the camera on it.

Rian thanked him and went back to the car with the disk. Leann had her department issued laptop running on the dash. They put the disk in and watched as Pauline Whitten walked up and put her card in the machine. Just after she entered her pin number her head lurched forward and she fell to the ground.

"Did you see that?" Rian said.

"Yeah, you can't see the bullet, but based on the entrance point it looks like maybe the strip mall across the highway. That's the only point of reference I see that fits."

"I agree. She wasn't standing straight at the ATM. She was half turned. That's why the other mall makes perfect sense."

Rian got out of the car and looked across the highway with her binoculars. "There's a shoe store in the middle there directly across from us," she said when she got back in the car and gunned the engine.

They pulled up in front of the shoe store and Leann was hanging up with the mall manager for that strip mall. "Are you scared of heights?" she asked.

"No," Leann said. "He's going to meet us in a few minutes. He said no one has been on this part of the roof in months. He did say they had the air conditioner repaired at the jewelry store, but that's at the other end of the mall."

"Make a note of that. This could be how he is gaining roof access. Maybe he's an a/c repair guy."

The manager showed up and let them through the door in the next store over that had a slim staircase that led to the roof. Rian walked every inch of the space twice. There was nothing, not a single trace that anyone had been up there.

"Look here," Leann said from a few feet away. Rian walked over to her.

"Look towards that ATM," Leann said as she handed her the binoculars.

"This is definitely where he was, within a few feet on either side," Rian said as she handed her back the binoculars. "There's nothing here. He's clean, well trained."

When they got back in the car, Rian wrote some notes on a piece of paper and handed it to Leann. "Call the manager back and get the name of that a/c repair place and the technician's name. Then, call Quinn and have him put together a radius of buildings around each of the shootings that pertain to our case. Then, call all of those companies to see if they had any air conditioning or other roof repairs done during or before the times of each shooting. We may have a huge lead here."

Chapter Fifteen

Rian finally gathered all of her Intel on Canturri and boxed it up. On the way to the post office she stopped for coffee and then stopped for gas. That's when she noticed a plain, dark blue car. She saw the same car behind her when she left her apartment complex. She also saw the car in the coffee shop drive-thru line, and now it was at the gas station a few pumps over. Rian got back in her car when she finished pumping gas. She hadn't seen anyone enter or exit the car, but when she pulled away the blue car pulled away too. Rian quickly dialed a number.

"Where are you?"

"I'm on my way to the morgue. Where are you?" Leann said.

"Do me a huge favor. Do you know the central post office on Fifth Street?"

"Yeah?"

"Meet me there. Go now. Call me when you get there."

"Okay, I'm only a few blocks from there. Is everything okay?"

"I think I have a tail and I need to take your car and you drive mine to the station so I can figure out who this is," Rian said.

"What the hell have you gotten into now, Rian," Leann said. "I'm here."

"Good, I'm pulling in too. There is a box in my back seat, take it in with you when you get to the station and lock it up," Rian said as she pulled up next to her.

Leann was standing outside of her car. Rian pulled up and jumped out.

"Okay, he's at the light and turning in now. Take my car and go. I'll follow in yours and see where he goes when he leaves you."

Rian got into Leann's car and watched her pull away in Rian's unmarked car. The blue car circled around and followed her without even noticing the driver change. Rian pulled out into the traffic a few car lengths behind him.

When her phone rang, she answered. "Do you see him?" Leann said.

"Yeah, he's in that blue rental behind you."

"Who is he?"

"I have no idea, but he's in for a rude awakening when I find out. Just go in like nothing's different and don't forget my box. I'll get it from you later."

"Okay."

"Call me when you get to your desk. I need to run the tag. It's definitely a rental car, but I need to see what company it is."

"Okay, I'm almost to the station," Leann said.

Rian pulled up against the curb a block away and watched the blue car park close to the station. She watched Leann get the box out of the backseat and walk inside. The blue car sped off and Rian pulled back out into the traffic. Rian followed him back to a small hotel and watched him go into a room on the first floor.

She quickly called the hotel and spoke in a high-pitched feminine voice. "Hi, I think my husband is in room one-twelve with some hussy. Can you tell me the name he checked in under?"

"I'm sorry, ma'am. We can't give out that information."

"If it was your wife with him wouldn't you want to know?" she pleaded.

"I don't think that is your husband ma'am. He's from Washington, D.C. and here on business."

Rian raised an eyebrow. What would a fed be doing following her? "Well, how long has that guy been staying in that room, because my husband is suppose to be gone on business to California and he left two days ago," she continued the crazy accent.

"That room has been booked since yesterday ma'am."

Rian hung up the phone and dialed Leann's number.

"Hey, I'm sorry. I got bombarded when I walked in. Apparently, Quinn is looking for you. The captain said they may have found something."

"That's fine, but right now I really don't give a flying fuck. Run this tag for me, Echo, Delta, Two, Bravo, One, Nine."

Leann typed a few keys on her laptop. "It's registered to Hertz," she said.

119

Rian hung up and called information to get the local branch phone number. She quickly dialed the number and waited for someone to pick up.

"This is Officer Owen with the Portland Police Department. One of your vehicles was just in a hit a run and the driver took off. A witness got the tag number and it's registered to you. I need to know who that is rented to please so I can file the report."

"Oh, yes ma'am," the guy said. Rian heard him typing keys after she read him the tag number.

"Here it is, that is a blue, two-thousand and twelve Impala. That car is rented under a government contract and we usually don't put individual drivers on the policy," he said. "Wait, it looks like the person that checked out the car did put a driver on the contract, it was probably one of our new people. His name is Joel Robbins and he has a Washington, D.C. driver's license. Do you want that number?"

"Thanks," Rian said as she wrote everything down. She hung up the phone and slammed her fist against the steering wheel. Why was Walsh having her followed? None of this made any sense. Hell, nothing made sense to her since the day he told her who Ari really was.

~

The next day Rian is sitting at her desk reading all of the information Detective Quinn obtained from all of the crime scenes. Whether or not she liked it, she was working an active case. She printed maps of each crime scene and highlighted the buildings in a three block radius that were having repairs done during the time frame of each shooting. There were at least three having air conditioner work done prior to the crimes. She was sure this was how he was operating. The only problem was she got the names of three different air conditioner companies. If the guy was using an alias she'd never be able to connect everything.

"Detective Casey, this came for you," a young officer handed her a brown envelope.

"Did you see who delivered it?" she asked when she recognized the package.

"A courier service, ma'am."

Rian sighed and opened the envelope when he walked away. She pulled out a cipher letter very similar to the first once she received.

QYHOLUKADRNEMDXATNVGPEWR.XYLOLUJ KQNZOAW
VTLODOUMDUECKH.TYGODUQWXEMRZEKW OAIRYNJEHD.
JTLHEEOYVAXRJEDCGOBMEIJNWGAFQOLRVYX OZU.
2.3326.3434.346.43633.

Rian read the numbers on the bottom. They key looked similar to the last one so she began writing out every other letter. When she finished she read the message.

YOU ARE IN DANGER. YOU KNOW TOO MUCH. YOU WERE WARNED. THEY ARE COMING FOR YOU.

She put the letter and scratch paper back into the envelope and set it inside her briefcase. She'd had enough of this cat and mouse game. The only way to get to the bottom of all of this was to go straight to the source. She booked a flight on her computer and told the captain she wasn't feeling well. He told her to take the next day off and he'd see her on Monday. He also told her he expected an update on this serial killer case Monday morning.

Rian had just enough time to throw some clothes in a bag and speed to the airport. Her flight was already boarding when she arrived. There was already a woman sitting in the window seat next to the first class aisle seat she was booked in. Rian pushed her bag under the seat in front of her and sat down. She ignored the woman next to her and watched in the mirrored lens she pulled from her pocket. Her tail had followed her onto the plane. She blew out a short breath and wondered how he was able to get a ticket so fast. She watched as he sat down a few rows back.

As the plane began to taxi the woman next to her moved closer. "You have bigger problems than Fiorino Canturri," she whispers. Rian stiffened. She knew that voice. It still shocked her when she saw Ari or heard her sweet voice. It was like a ghost from the grave appearing over and over.

"What do you mean?" Rian said quietly without looking at her.

"They've been after me for a while, now they're after you," Ari whispered.

"Who?" Rian questioned, still watching the man in the lens.

"The FBI."

"That's crazy. They're only after you if you're connected to your father. Are you?" Rian finally looked at her. She was wearing brown contacts and her long blond hair was still dyed brown. The beautiful, vibrant, young woman she was in love with was buried somewhere under that disguise. Rian wondered if that woman died the night Ari supposedly died in her arms.

"No, of course not. I'm connected to you. When my father threatened to kill you, I agreed to let him fake my death and went home to be the good little daughter the day after the funeral. About three months later Philip Walsh met with my father at his compound in Buenos Aires."

"Walsh?" Rian paused. "How do you know this?"

"I was there," Ari said as she turned towards the window to watch them fly through the clouds. "They're after me because I witnessed the exchange. I was on the grounds when Walsh was being escorted out. He didn't recognize me at first, but my father introduced me. I know he had only seen me once or twice with you, but he must have realized I was the same woman you buried," she said softly.

"So you're telling me Philip Walsh is working with your father?"

"Yes, and they are trying to kill you because I know and they think I will tell you. So, they are also after you. Now, you know. You can't meet Walsh."

"Walsh said he has a plan to set your father up using U.S. Customs."

Ari shook her head. "That's how they are working together, except it's not a set up. He told you that to see if you knew anything about it. He was setting you up. When you went to my father's compound that sent them all scurrying like rats. They had to figure out how much you knew."

Rian sat back and stretched her legs out. "How long have you been following me," she asked.

"Long enough to know that Medical Examiner's in love with you," Ari said.

"Why come back if your father wants me dead? Why risk it?"

"Because I love you, Rian. I never realized you were going to ask me to marry you. My father thinks you took me from him and I betrayed him by lying with one of the people trying to take him down. That was the ultimate betrayal in his eyes," she said quietly.

Rian wanted to close her eyes and wake up again like the movie Groundhog Day, only start the year over instead of the day.

"Do you love her?" Ari asked.

"Losing you nearly killed me, Ari," Rian said without looking at her.

Ari wiped the tears that fell from her eyes. "I'm sorry," she whispered.

"You should have told me the truth."

"Would you have dated me if you knew who I was?" Ari questioned knowing the answer.

"Up until a few months ago, I only knew Canturri had a daughter. I didn't know a name, or even a real age. I barely knew anything about you during my investigation," she paused. "I guess if you had said Canturri was your last name I would've thrown you in an interrogation room until you told me everything about him," Rian said as she rolled her head towards the window. It was so weird hearing the voice and looking at the person next to her. It just didn't match.

"I knew you were an agent. I tried to stay away from you, but I fell in love with you and that was it. I let my past go."

Rian looked past Ari at the blue sky in the window. "No," she said.

"No?" Ari questioned.

"No, I don't love her," Rian looked at Ari's brown eyes briefly before turning away again.

"What are you going to do?"

"Get you the hell away from them, the FBI and your father. Then, I will figure a way out of this mess," Rian closed her eyes.

"You haven't been sleeping have you?" Ari asked. "I can see in your eyes how tired you are."

"I've been through nine months of hell, it's not exactly easy to sleep," Rian said with a yawn.

Ari watched her body relax as lulling of the plane put her to sleep. She wanted to wrap her arms around her, but knew better. Rian hadn't touched her once since learning she was still alive. That hurt, but she understood. She couldn't really expect her to go running into her arms after everything she went through. She watched as Rian slept for over an hour. When she started to move and jerk in her sleep Ari grabbed her hand and held it in her own. Rian calmed immediately. Ari wiped a tear from her cheek with her other hand.

Rian finally woke up and noticed their locked hands and quickly let go. She wasn't ready to have Ari back and this stranger next to her wasn't Ari. She stretched out and sat up.

"When we land I am going to get off alone. I want you to go straight to the nearest ticket counter and book us on the next flight back to Portland. I have to get rid of this fed. I'll meet you at the gate when it's time to board," Rian said.

"Be careful, Rian. These people want you dead."

"I'll be fine," Rian reached over and squeezed her hand before letting go.

As soon as the plane landed, Ari did as instructed. Rian led the guy straight past baggage claim where she got into a taxi. She paid the guy to drive around town and come back to the airport. She watched the fed wave a taxi over as they drove off. It took a few blocks, but eventually she no longer saw the cab behind them. When they pulled back up at the airport she tipped the driver and waited to see him show back up. After a few minutes, she went inside and checked the flight board. The next flight to Portland was leaving in two hours. She walked upstairs and sat behind a small planted tree where she could watch the entrance doors and path to the terminals. If Agent Joel Robbins came back looking for her she'd see him. She waited until it was the final boarding call for her flight. Thankfully, she hadn't seen him. She went through security and ran to the gate.

"You have my ticket waiting for me," she told the attendant at the gate.

"I have our tickets," she heard the sweet voice and turned around. "I wanted to make sure you didn't miss the flight," Ari said.

Rian handed the attendant their tickets and they quickly boarded. "I didn't think you were coming back. I got worried," Ari said as she sat by the window in their first class row.

"I had to make sure we weren't followed back," Rian said.

When the plane left the ground, her mind began racing. She had to form a plan to stop all of this and keep Ari safe and she had to do it fast. Once the fed realized he'd definitely lost her and she didn't show up to meet Walsh he'd be out for blood himself. He'd know she knew the truth. She had no idea how high up the ladder this went and she was praying it started and stopped at Walsh.

"What's the plan now," Ari asked.

Rian looked at the brunette next to her and shook her head at the contrast. "We get them before they get us," she said.

Chapter Sixteen

After the plane landed, Rian used the nearest payphone to call Leann. She asked her to come pick her up at the airport and not tell anyone where she's going and what she's doing and watch for a tail. Leann was confused. She thought Rian was on her floor working in her closet sized office. She was even more confused when she pulled up at the airport and Rian was standing on the curb with a petite brunette.

"What's going on, Rian?" Leann said as Rian and the woman both got into her car.

"Drive," Rian said as she watched behind them to see if anyone was following.

"Where are we going? What the hell?" Leann shook her head and drove off.

"The less you know the better." Rian turned back around satisfied they hadn't picked up a tail.

Leann glanced in the rearview mirror. The brunette in the backseat was staring out the side window. She wondered what Rian had gotten herself into and how it involved the mysterious woman. She had no idea where to go so she just kept driving.

"Where going to the Governor," Rian said. When Leann looked at her with raised eyebrows Rian shook her head. "The hotel," she huffed. "The Governor Hotel."

Leann laughed. "Downtown?"

"Yeah."

They rode the rest of the way in silence. Rian constantly kept watch on their surroundings. So far they were clear, but it wouldn't be long before the FBI was back on their trail. When they pulled up at the front of the hotel Rian got out.

"I'll be right back," she said to both of the women in the car as she shut the door.

Leann looked in the mirror again and the woman was watching Rian walk away. She wanted to speak to her, but she had no idea what to say so she sat quietly. Rian returned a few minutes later.

"We're in room three-fifteen," she said as she opened Ari's door and waved for her to get out. "I really don't want to involve you, Leann, but I have no other choice."

"Whatever you need, Rian, just tell me. I said I would always help you."

"Go to my apartment quickly use the siren if you have to. There are two locked file boxes under my bed, get them both," Rian looked back at Ari. "And go get a bottle of hair color remover. Come back here as soon as you have everything. Room three-fifteen."

"Okay," Leann said.

"If you see anyone watching you or it looks like you're being followed don't come back here, go straight to the station and call from a payphone somewhere. Don't use your cell phone either." Rian paused. "And Leann, please be careful. These people are dangerous."

Leann nodded and drove off.

"She'd go into the gates of hell if you asked her to," Ari said as they walked inside the hotel. "It's because she loves you, I know the feeling."

"Ari, please." Rian sighed as the elevator doors closed.

When they walked into the room the first thing Ari noticed was the double beds. There was a chair, small couch, and coffee table by the window on the opposite side of the room. She took her coat off and laid it across the nearest bed. "This is nice," she said.

"This might be the only comfort we get for a while," Rian said as she grabbed the room service menu. "Are you hungry?"

"Starving," Ari walked over and peeked at the menu. "A burger sounds good," she said.

Rian turned her head and looked at the brown eyes staring back at her. She knew Ari was being honest with her, but it was extremely difficult to trust her after everything she found out once the truth surfaced. One thing she knew for certain, Fiorino Canturri and the FBI would never hurt Ari again, not as long as she was alive. Rian closed the menu and called down for two burgers.

When the elevator bell dinged she moved quickly to the door and watched through the peephole. The room service cart stopped at their door. Rian opened the door and watched the guy's every move as he pushed the cart inside and uncovered the two dinner plates. She handed him a five-dollar bill on his way out.

"What's your plan?" Ari said between bites.

"We need to get out of the country undetected. Walsh has a long reach and a lot of puppets that will do whatever he says without question. He'll be back on our trail soon, which is why we need the trail to end." Rian put the lid on the remnants of her dinner and stood up. She watched the cars passing on the street below. The sun had faded and the streetlights were coming on.

"How are we going to end the trail?" Ari asked from behind her.

Rian turned back around. She jumped when she heard a soft knock on the door. She crossed the room in a few steps and checked the peephole. Leann was standing there looking up and down the hall. She pulled the door open and ushered her inside.

Leann handed her the two large file boxes and the plastic bag from the store. Rian set the boxes on the coffee table and handed the bag to Ari. She walked back to the window as Ari went into the bathroom.

"I'm sorry I had to involve you in this," she said.

"Rian, I've been involved for some time now. I wish you would just tell me what's going on."

"Sit down," Rian said as she waved her hand towards the couch. Leann sat in the chair and watched Rian pace the floor.

"I found out recently that my former boss with the FBI is working with Fiorino Canturri. He's helping him bring guns into the States."

"Holy shit," Leann said.

"They know that I know." Rian paused and stopped pacing. "They're trying to kill me."

"Oh my god, Rian. Isn't there someone you can call to turn him in, someone you trust?"

Rian shook her head. "I have no idea how high up the chain this goes. I don't know who is involved. Hell, I'm not even sure how long it's been going on. At this point you're the only one I can trust."

"What are you going to do?" Leann asked.

Rian sat on the couch. "The only thing I *can* do," she said. "Fake my death and go after these bastards."

"So, that's our plan?" Ari asked from the doorway. Rian jumped. It was like looking at a ghost when she saw Ari's blond hair and different colored eyes. It was one thing to hear the voice, but to physically see her again was almost too much for Rian to handle. Her heart raced and her hands shook.

Rian cleared her throat and forced her nerves to calm down. "Leann, this is Arianna Canturri."

Leann gasped.

Ari walked into the room and sat down next to Rian on the couch.

"I also found out recently that Ari's father faked her death and threatened to kill me if she didn't go with him."

"Wow," Leann said. She couldn't help staring at the beautiful woman sitting next to Rian.

Ari smiled and stuck her hand out. Leann politely shook it.

"Special Agent Walsh is trying to kill Ari because she witnessed the transaction between himself and her father.

He also knows she told me everything. He has FBI agents following us all over the place," Rian watched the changes in Leann's face as she took in everything Rian was saying to her. "I know it's a lot to take in. I feel like I've been on a rollercoaster over the past few weeks."

Leann shook her head. "This is crazy."

"Tell me about it." Rian looked at Leann, then at Ari and smiled softly. "I have to keep her safe. That son of a bitch took her from me once and it's not going to happen again. As far as I'm concerned, Walsh and Canturri can rot in hell together."

"I second that," Ari said.

"What a mess," Leann laughed slightly. "I never realized you came with such dramatic baggage, Rian."

"I told you, you didn't want to know about me, didn't I?" Rian shrugged.

Leann nodded. "Yes, numerous times as I recall. So, how are you going to stop them if you can't get any authorities involved?"

"Walsh tried to find out what I knew when he was here recently by telling me of a plan to set-up Canturri soon. I'm assuming he was telling me the truth about meeting with Canturri soon, even though he was lying about the whole set-up. My goal is to catch them together."

"How are you going to do that?"

"They think we are on the run, so I plan to fake our deaths and hide out until we know when they plan to meet," Rian said.

"How are we going to fake our deaths?" Ari asked.

Rian looked at Leann and took a deep breath. "Here's where your skills come in handy," she said.

Leann raised an eyebrow and waited.

"I need two Jane Doe's," Rian said.

Leann nodded. She was putting her career on the line, but she knew of two bodies she could possibly sneak out of the morgue that had been unclaimed for a number of months.

"I don't want to give you too many details. Just meet us at Mulino Airport tomorrow morning at five a.m. with the cadavers." Rian said. Leann nodded and Rian handed her a paper bag. "Dress them in these clothes," she said. "I also need you to bring a couple of new syringes and empty vacutainer tubes."

"Okay," Leann made a small note in her phone. "Anything else?"

"Go to the sporting goods store and get a small wet-dry backpack big enough to fit both of my file boxes. A floating one would be great, but whatever you can find will do, and two large emergency blankets. They're silver and usually folded really small. Also, get some water tablets and a drinking bottle. And pay cash for everything."

"Got it," Leann said.

"When we take off I want you to take everything out of my apartment and torch it."

"Are you sure?"

"Yes, everything."

"Okay," she looked at Rian. "Do you know how to fly a plane?"

134

Rian nodded. "You'd be surprised what the government taught me how to do."

"Do you guys need anything else before I go?" Leann asked as she stood up.

"No," Rian walked her to the door. "Thank you for doing this."

Leann smiled. "I said I wanted to help," she said as she walked away.

"What are you planning to do with the bodies and the blood?" Ari asked when Rian sat back down.

"We are going to die in a plane crash," she said simply.

~

Ari fell asleep and Rian walked over to the window. She watched the lights below and silently wiped the tears that fell. She was happy to have Ari back, but she still hurt for the person she lost. Even with Ari alive and in the same room she couldn't stop the grieving. She hoped her plan worked and they would get their lives back. If not, she'd die fighting. She turned to look at the sleeping figure in the bed and realized Ari was standing behind her. She turned around and wrapped her arms around the smaller woman and pulled her tightly against her. Ari reached up and wiped the wet tears from Rian's face.

"I'm sorry for all of the pain I put you through," Ari said through her own tears. "Watching you at my funeral nearly killed me. I hated my father so much for what he did to you, to me, to us. I couldn't take it anymore when I saw what his men did to you. That's why I had to go find you. I had to make sure you were okay. I tried to warn you."

Rian wiped Ari's tears with the back of her hand and kissed her wet cheek. "You sent me those letters?"

"Yes."

Rian smiled. "Very creative."

Ari smiled that same bright smile Rian remembered over and over in her dreams. "I've missed you so much," Rian sighed and held her tightly.

Ari closed her eyes and silently prayed to stay in that position for the rest of her life. She felt so loved and so safe in Rian's arms.

Chapter Seventeen

At two o'clock in the morning Ari felt Rian shaking and heard her talking in her sleep.

"No," Rian said over and over. "Please, Ari no," she cried.

"Wake up. Rian, wake up." Ari said as she held onto her.

When Rian opened her eyes and saw Ari she jumped back and nearly fell out the bed. Her heart was racing and she was shaking uncontrollably. Ari slowly moved towards her.

"It's okay. I'm right here, baby," she said softly.

Rian got up and drank a glass of water and splashed cold water on her face. When she walked back towards the bed Ari was sitting there with the sheet wrapped around her. Rian closed her eyes and opened them again. Ari was still sitting there.

"I keep dreaming about you dying over and over again. I used to have horrible nightmares and since you've been back they've come back too," she said as she sat down next to Ari.

"I'm so sorry, Rian." Ari wrapped her arms around her and held her tight. "I should have told you the truth instead of listening to my father. I was just so scared he would hurt you," she sighed. "I turned out to be the one that hurt you."

Rian backed away and looked into her eyes. "You didn't hurt me, Ari. Your father did, and he will pay for everything he's done."

Both women jumped when the phone on the nightstand rang loudly. Rian picked it up on the second ring.

"The captain's been looking all over for you," Leann said. "Steven Monahan was pulled over earlier tonight just outside of Portland. He had a tail light out on his repair van and when the officer ran his license, it was flagged of course. He arrested him and held him until Quinn got there. He had a .308 caliber hunting rifle with a high powered scope in the van," she said enthusiastically.

"Wow, that's great," Rian said.

"It looks like he has a wife and a child according to the pictures in his wallet and apparently he's living outside of Yakima," she said.

"Everything they have is circumstantial at most. I hope it sticks."

"Quinn's on the way to his house with a search warrant. That's why the captain was looking for you. I told him you were sick and probably turned your phone off," Leann said.

"I tossed that phone at Dulles Airport," Rian said.

Leann laughed. "Always the agent. I think it's embedded in your bones or something."

"Maybe," Rian said.

"You solved this case."

"No, you did, Leann. I just helped you along."

"We did it together. We make a good team," Leann said.

"Yeah, I'm going to miss working with you a little bit," Rian said.

"Only a little bit?" Leann teased. "I wish we could go out and celebrate. Instead, I'm thawing bodies in the middle of the night."

"Where are you calling from?" Rian asked.

"A payphone. I know the drill. Get some sleep. I'll see you in a few hours."

When Rian hung the phone up Ari was sitting next to her. "Tonight they picked up the only suspect in a serial killer case we were working together," Rian said.

"Oh, that's good. You're good at what you do," Ari smiled. "Your intelligence and confidence are what drew me to you in the first place."

Rian raised an eyebrow. "I thought it was my looks and my charm."

Ari grinned. "That too."

~

When Ari woke up again Rian was standing at the window fully dressed sipping a cup of coffee. "I'd say good morning, but I'm not sure how good it really is," Rian said hearing Ari get out of bed.

"Every morning I wake up with you is a good morning to me," Ari said as she walked past Rian and into the bathroom.

Ari finished her shower and dried her hair. She finished dressing, poured a cup of coffee, and sat down. "What time do we need to leave?"

"The car's already here. I'm just waiting for you."

"Why didn't you say something, Rian?" Ari said as she stood up and closed her small bag.

Rian shrugged. "There was no need to rush you. Is there anything in that bag you can't live without?"

"No, why?"

"You'll never see it again. Make sure your wallet and I.D. are in there," Rian said as she grabbed her own bag and walked towards the door. Ari quickly followed.

~

When the taxi pulled up on the backside of the airport Rian handed him a hundred dollar bill and she and Ari got out. The black M.E. van was parked nearby. The taxi drove out of sight before they walked over to the van.

"I need to go check in. I believe that is our plane over there," Rian nodded in the direction of a white small single engine Piper aircraft with a thin red stripe down the side.

Ari and Leann watched her walk away.

"She cares for you, you know," Ari said.

Leann nodded. "She loves you," she said.

Ari looked at her. "She's different since you've been back, less broken," Leann said to her.

"Thank you for helping her, for helping us," Ari said.

Leann smiled. "Someone needed to be her friend. I'm glad it was me."

Rian returned a few minutes later. "Okay, we're all set. Drive over to that plane and park close by. We'll unload everything without them noticing, hopefully."

Leann positioned the van next to the plane and opened the side doors. She and Rian slid both of the bodies into the plane one at a time. The four-seater plane only had two seats in it and the rest of the space created a very small compartment behind the front two seats for luggage and supplies. They piled the two bodies in the compartment on top of Rian and Ari's sparse luggage and put a blanket over them.

"Did you bring the other stuff?" Rian asked. Leann nodded and handed her a sealed plastic bag.

"I need you to draw two tubes of blood from each of us," Rian said as she held her arm out.

"I haven't done this on a living person in ten years," Leann said as she tied the rubber band around Rian's arm and stuck her. Rian flinched. "I'm sorry," she said.

Rian watched the small tube fill up. Leann quickly replaced it with a second tube. She did the same thing to Ari, careful not to stick her as hard. She finished and Ari climbed into the co-pilot seat and put her seatbelt on.

"I'll get word to you when I can. Watch your mail and don't believe what the news reports, but make sure everyone thinks you do," Rian said as she hugged her quickly. "Thank you for everything, Leann."

"You're welcome. Please be careful," she said.

Leann got back in the van and drove over to the hangar to wait and watch them take off.

Rian put the headphones on and pushed the choke on the dash. The little plane sputtered to life. She idled the engine for a minute to warm it up.

"Tower, this is Hotel, eight, seven, four, three requesting an open runway for takeoff, over," Rian said into the headset.

"Eight, seven, four, three, tower, you're cleared for runway 1B, over."

"Here we go," Rian said to Ari as she engaged the throttle. They began slowly bouncing towards the open strip. When they reached the end Rian pushed the throttle back and the plane picked up speed. When they reached the middle, Rian pulled back on the yolk and the little plane slowly lifted off the ground. She climbed the plane to five-thousand feet and leveled out.

"Eight, seven, four, three, tower, you're unscheduled so your ceiling is ten-thousand, over."

"Tower, eight, seven, four, three, roger on ten-thousand," Rian said as she climbed the plane to seven-thousand feet and leveled off again. She set the autopilot to fly north at the same speed and altitude and opened the map.

"It's going to take about two hours," Rian said to Ari through the headset.

"Where are we going?" Ari asked.

"Canada," Rian said.

Ari nodded and watched the blue sky in front of them. It was so peaceful flying through the clouds with nothing else around. The headset drowned out most of the noise from the engine. They hit turbulence and Ari gripped the seat with both hands as the tiny plane shook. Rian smiled and pulled back on the yolk slightly to push them a little higher away from the turbulence.

An hour into their flight Rian set the autopilot on the coordinates she chose and got up from her seat. Ari watched her shift the bodies around to open a small compartment door at the very back of the plane. She pulled out a small black backpack and put it to the side.

"What's that?" Ari said when Rian sat back down and put her headset back on.

"Parachute," Rian said. Ari's eyes grew large. "When we cross the border soon we are going to put them in our places and I'm going to set the autopilot to fly back into Washington and crash. We're going to jump out over the Strait of Georgia and swim to shore before we freeze to death."

Ari nodded and swallowed the lump in her throat. "I trust you," she said.

~

"Are you sure about this?" Ari asked as she watched Rian spread the blood from the tubes all over the plane in areas that wouldn't burn as easily. She knew the bodies would burn beyond recognition because of the alcohol used to clean the bodies and the formaldehyde used to preserve them.

"Yeah, they'll see the plane was rented to me and when they find our blood and I.D.'s they'll think we died," Rian said. When she finished she put the tubes in her pocket and began putting the bodies in the seats. She put the seatbelts around them to hold them up and placed the headsets on their heads.

"Are you ready?" Rian asked Ari as she programmed the autopilot to climb back up to seven-thousand feet and run for an hour. When it stopped running the plane would crash into the National Forrest in Washington State and burst into flames. Or at least, that was her plan.

Ari nodded and waited for Rian to put on the backpack. She hooked the tandem straps around Ari and snapped them to her straps. Then, she clipped the small backpack to her straps.

"Here we go," she yelled as she pulled the door open just enough for them to fit through it. They were just above five-thousand feet. Rian held onto Ari tightly and jumped into the wind.

They spiraled at over a hundred miles an hour as they quickly fell through the sky. Rian counted in her head using her training to evaluate when they hit three-thousand feet. When she got to the bingo number she pulled the cord and the parachute flew out of the backpack and filled the sky above them like a large red and blue balloon. Ari jerked against her as the chute cut their fall speed in half. Rian grabbed the side cords and began looking for a landing spot away from people. She found the water next to the mountains and directed their descent in that direction.

A few seconds later, they hit the water with a huge splash. Rian unclipped Ari and pushed her to the surface as she sank down with the parachute on her back. It took her longer than she wanted to get out of the straps and swim away from all of the material to get to the surface. Ari was bobbing ten feet away frantically searching for her.

"I'm over here," Rian yelled as she swam towards her. The water was cold, but the shore was only a few feet away. Rian looked back, thankful the parachute sank to the bottom. Hopefully, no one saw them come down.

Ari's teeth chattered. "I didn't see you come up. I thought...-"

"I'm okay," Rian said. "Just swim as fast as you can baby. We have to get out of this water."

They reached the shore and Rian crawled out of the water and turned around. Ari's face was blue and she was shivering. Rian grabbed her and pulled her out of the water.

"I'd rather die like this, than at the hands of my father." Ari was shaking so bad she could barely talk.

Rian wrapped her arms around her. She knew hypothermia was setting in. She needed to get Ari warm and soon. She walked her up into the woods and opened the backpack. She quickly opened the emergency blanket.

"Strip your wet clothes off and wrap up in this," she said to Ari as she did the same. They huddled together in the warming blankets. Rian had their clothes hanging in a tree a few feet away.

"Do you think our clothes will dry?" Ari asked. She was still cold, but wasn't shivering uncontrollably anymore.

"Probably not completely, but they will be dry enough for us to move tonight."

Chapter Eighteen

Rian and Ari hiked most of the night through the mountains in their damp clothes. When the sun came up they were cold and hungry and had another mile to go before they finally found a town.

"We need to get moving," Rian said as she used the phone inside the gas station to call a taxi service.

"We need some dry clothes," Ari said back to her. She was huddled in the corner by the heater. "What's the next step in the plan?" she asked. Rian walked over to her and held her hands out to warm them.

"Our taxi's here," Rian grabbed her hand and hurried to the waiting car. "I'll explain everything soon. I promise," Rian ran the back of her hand over Ari's warm cheek.

"Take us to the Pacific Central Station, please," Rian said as she pulled Ari against her to try and keep her warm.

Both women watched the beautiful trees and buildings go by as they drove through Vancouver to the train station. Rian kept note of certain places as they neared the station. She handed the driver a handful of Canadian

Dollars that she exchanged her U.S. Dollars for in the store where she made the phone call.

"Wait here. I'll be right back," she said to the driver and Ari who stared back at her through the open window.

Rian moved quickly inside the train station. She'd only been there once and that was half a dozen years ago. She maneuvered through the thin crowd towards the ticket area and luggage lockers. She went down each row until she came to number nineteen-nineteen. She pulled the chain she had hidden under her shirt. A small silver key was on the other end. She stuck the key in the lock and the door popped open revealing a small container. Rian looked in both directions, satisfied no one was watching her she opened the container and put all of its contents in her inside jacket pocket. She closed the container and relocked the locker before hurrying over to the ticket line.

"Two person cabin on the Canadian, please," Rian said to the woman behind the glass. She watched her type on her computer. When she asked for I.D. and payment Rian handed her two cards from the contents in her pocket. One was a Canadian I.D. with her picture on it and the name Olivia Dawson on it. She also handed her a Visa card with the same name. The woman input the information and ran the card. She smiled and handed both cards back to Rian along with two train tickets. She was thankful for some of the things she learned while working as a government agent. One of the biggest was having a safe place in another country in case you were ever compromised.

Rian rushed outside and got back in the waiting car. "I saw a street market a few blocks over there," Rian pointed North. "You can drop us off there."

Ari watched Rian pull a map out of her pocket. It was marked in various places in red pen with notes written on the side margin. She folded it and put it back in her pocket when the car stopped in front of the large indoor flea market style shopping center. Rian handed him a few more bills and got out of the car. She held her hand out to Ari.

"Let's go shopping," Rian said as they walked inside. "We need a few changes of clothes, toiletries, and a suitcase. Get something warm and comfortable."

"What were you doing at the train station?" Ari asked as she started down the first aisle.

"I'll explain everything later. We need to hurry our train leaves in less than three hours," Rian said as she grabbed two pairs of jeans and a sweater from one of the tables. She also picked up a suitcase big enough for their clothes and the backpack she'd been carrying. She watched Ari move around the booth looking at the various clothing items for sale.

An hour later they had walked the entire market. They quickly changed and packed their suitcase in the restroom. They tossed their old clothes in the trashcan and brushed the fur off their teeth.

"I feel somewhat better," Ari smiled.

"Me too. I have one more thing to do, then we can grab something to eat and head back to the train station." Rian led them towards the market exit.

~

Rian and Ari boarded the train and made their way down the narrow hallway towards cabin number twelve. Rian opened the door to a seven foot by four foot room with two fold down bunks against the wall and two small chairs against the window. There was a small closet on one side with drinking water, towels, pillows, sheets, blankets, and a small compartment for luggage. The other side of the room had a small door that led to a tiny bathroom with a toilet and a sink. Ari walked in and sat in one the chairs. The room was small, but cozy enough for two people.

"Dinner will be served in the dining car in two hours. If you paid for in-room meals they will be distributed once the dining car opens for service," the conductor said as he walked down the hallway.

Ari watched Rian store their suitcase and sit in the chair next to her. "I'm sorry I couldn't tell you anything. I have no idea if we're being followed, so I have to take every precaution."

"I understand," Ari said. "I trust you, Rian. I am a little curious though. We pretty much left everything behind in that plane."

Rian grinned. "Blame the American government or at this point thank them," she said as she stretched her legs out and turned the cabin heater on full blast. "One of the first things they teach you is how to survive if you're ever compromised. You need a safety net in another country.

A little over six years ago I traveled around Canada and I decided to make it my safety net. I purchased a baggage locker at the train station and stashed a fake Canadian I.D., a prepaid Visa, a map of the country with personal marks about certain places I've been that are safe, and a few other items. I never thought I'd need to access that locker."

"Wow. You're like 007 or something," Ari laughed.

Rian shook her head. "No. More like a model FBI agent that did everything by the book and a paranoid retired agent that's trying to stay alive."

"Well either way, I am glad you followed the book. What was that package you mailed?"

"A throw away cell phone with instructions."

"Who did you send it to?"

"Leann," Rian said. She watched the slight change in Ari's face. "I'll call the phone in a day or two since we have some time before we get to our destination. Hopefully, she can give me some updated information."

"What is our destination?"

"Toronto. We arrive in about three and a half days. Then, we cross the border."

"We're going back to the States?" Ari raised an eyebrow.

"Washington, D.C. actually," Rian stated nonchalantly. She watched out the window as the train pulled away from the station.

"Isn't that a little crazy, Rian?"

"No. Not really, as long as Walsh thinks we're dead. I'll be able to get close."

"You're not going to follow him are you?"

Rian nodded. "I have to catch him meeting with your father. It's the only way to take them both down."

"What are you going to do if you catch them together?"

"I don't know yet," Rian looked at her. "Do you care about your father, Ari?" Rian paused. "Should I call you Arianna?"

"I've always been Ari to you and always will be."

"For the record, I think Arianna is a beautiful name. It fits you well. What's your middle name?"

"Francina."

"That's pretty too."

"Thank you." Ari smiled. "How do you think I feel about my father?"

Rian shrugged.

"He took away the only thing that ever mattered to me in this world." Ari grabbed Rian's hand. "Whatever he has coming to him won't be enough as far as I'm concerned."

Rian nodded and squeezed her hand. She honestly wasn't sure how she was going to end this fiasco, but one thing was for sure, Philip Walsh and Fiorino Canturri would never be able to hurt her or Ari ever again, she would make sure of that.

~

Two days later Rian pulled the throw away cell phone out of her pocket. It was identical to the one she sent

Leann. She dialed the programmed number and waited as it rang.

"Hello," Leann answered skeptically.

"It's Rian."

"Oh my god! Finally, I was starting to worry," Leann said as she rushed out the building towards a spot outside where she could talk without being overheard.

"How is everything?" Rian asked.

"Hectic, crazy. Your funerals are both Thursday. The captain went a little overboard, I think he secretly had a crush on you," she laughed.

"So the plan worked?"

"Oh yeah. They found the plane wreckage and bodies the next day and they were sent to a lab in Washington that confirmed both identities. It was all over the news."

"Perfect," Rian said a silent prayer that her plan was working so far. "Did you do everything else that I asked?"

"Yes. As soon as you guys were airborne I went to your place and took out all of the stuff on your list and torched it in the incinerator," Leann said. "Where are you guys?"

"Canada."

"What's next in your plan?"

"I can't give you any more information, Leann. They may come question you and you know too much as it is. Just know that we are safe. Call the news reporters and have one of them film the services or at least take pictures. I need to see who attends both. Throw that phone in the incinerator when you hang up with me. I'll call you in a couple days on the other phone I sent you."

"What if I don't hear from you?"

"Then I'm dead."

"Be careful, Rian."

"Always," Rian said before she hung up.

"Well?" Ari said.

"We're officially dead. Our funerals are this Thursday."

"I've died twice and had two funerals in one year. There should be some kind of record for that or something," Ari said sarcastically.

"The good thing is so far everyone's buying it. Leann said it was all over the news. The clincher will be if Walsh shows up at the service. I know your father will probably avoid a trip to the States. He may send someone though."

"It will be my brother probably," Ari said.

"Brother?"

"Valentino Canturri's my half-brother. He's ten years older than me. How did you not know about him?"

"Our records indicated Valentino was Fiorino's nephew, not his son," Rian said.

"Val's an asshole and he's my father's right-hand. He has been groomed to take over since he was old enough to talk. If anyone from my father's organization shows up it will be Val."

"Is he the one that set up your death?"

"Yeah. Well my father met with me face to face. When I agreed he left the country and Val handled all of the details. He's smart, I'll give him that, but he's as corrupt as my father if not worse. I know as my father's right-hand he's personally killed numerous people. Val's dangerous," Ari said.

"I guess I didn't have the Intel on your father that I thought I did if I didn't even know about his two grown children. One of which I was living my life with," Rian shook her head. "I think Walsh may have been proofreading my Intel before it came to me. That son of a bitch, I wonder how long he's been working with your father."

"I have no idea. I'd never seen him before when I met him with you, but I was gone for over two years. Maybe it happened during that time," she shrugged.

A knock at the door startled both of them. Rian jumped up and checked the peephole. She opened it when she saw the server waiting patiently with the dinner service cart.

"Filet mignon with mixed vegetables for two with cheesecake for dessert and two glasses of red wine," the woman said as she handed everything to Rian.

"I was starting to wonder if they had forgotten us tonight," Ari said as she folded the table down from the wall next to the chairs.

Chapter Nineteen

The train lurched to a stop at union Station in Toronto. Rian grabbed their suitcase and ushered Ari towards the exit car. They walked briskly through the station and hailed a taxi outside. Rian looked at the red marks on her map and directed him to a nearby hotel.

"I need to regroup," she said to Ari.

"It will be nice to be immobile for a little bit. I feel like I'm still on the train."

"Me too," Rian said. "It'll pass."

After they checked into the hotel Rian took a long hot shower to wash away the week of grit and grime that was stuck to her skin. The hot warm water flowing down her back sent her mind back in time. She physically missed Ari. They hadn't made love since Ari returned to her and Rian knew she was the one holding back. She loved her so much and was so happy to have her back in her life, but every time she touched Ari, she was reminded of the night she lost her.

When Rian came out of the bathroom in a robe Ari went straight to the shower. Rian grabbed a new throw away phone from their suitcase and dialed the programmed number. She was relieved when Leann picked up.

"How were the funerals?" she joked.

"Sad," Leann said.

"I'm sorry you had to deal with that." Rian paused and walked over to the window. Their room was on the seventh floor and the view of downtown Toronto was breathtaking. "Did you get any pictures or video?"

"Yes. A news photographer owed me a favor. He got about a hundred photos."

"Great."

"I also overhead a weird conversation between the FBI Agent named Walsh and another guy."

"So, Walsh was definitely there?" Rain asked.

"Oh yeah, he spoke. They pretty much did both funerals together and he stayed for the whole thing."

"That rat bastard." Rian paced the floor. "What did you hear him say?"

"He was sitting alone for the service, but when it was over he was walking with another man with dark hair. I was parked in that direction so I pretended to be upset and crying like everyone else as I walked along close to them. Walsh told the other guy to tell his dad he'd see him soon and he turned away and went in another direction."

"Hmm, I bet that was Val," Rian said to herself.

"Who's Val?" Leann asked.

"Ari's brother."

Leann laughed. "And the plot thickens."

"No kidding," Rian said. "Are the pictures on a disk?"

"Yeah, do you have a way to see it where you are?"

"No. Damn it," Rian said. "Wait, can you print a few of them?"

"Yes, my printer prints photos in the lab." Leann said.

"Okay, print the ones of Walsh and everyone he talked to especially the dark-haired guy," Rian said. She gave her the address to a P.O. Box close by to send them to. "Do the same thing with this phone that you did with the last."

"When will I hear from you again?" Leann said.

"When this is all over," Rian said as she hung up.

~

Rian had her back to the bathroom door when she heard it click. She turned around to see Ari standing a few feet away wearing only a white thick terrycloth robe. Her blond hair cascaded down her shoulders and her two different eyes were shining brightly in the dim light. She smiled softly. She was just as beautiful as the day Rian met her.

Rian crossed the room and stopped in front of her. She reached down and pulled the belt loose keeping her eyes on Ari's as the robe opened. She pushed it back off Ari's shoulders, bent her head slightly, and kissed her. It had been so long since she tasted the sweet, softness of Ari's mouth. She ran her tongue around the edge of her lips before slipping inside. Ari matched her pace dueling for position and gasping for air.

Rian felt like she could breathe again. She pulled Ari against her and picked her up. Ari wrapped her legs around her as Rian walked them back towards the bed. Rian could feel how wet Ari was when she laid her on the bed and rubbed her stomach between Ari's spread legs as she moved up to kiss her again.

Ari ran her hands up Rian's back and into her short hair as she wrapped her legs around her and rolled Rian onto her back. She sat up and straddled Rian as she moved back and forth slowly spreading her wetness all over her stomach. Rian ran her hands up Ari's thighs to her slim waist and cupped her small breasts. Ari moaned softly as she bent down and kissed Rian. She continued to move against Rian's stomach while their tongues tangled behind their sealed lips.

Ari pulled away slightly breaking the kiss. Rian was panting. Ari grinned and stretched out on top of her. Rian spread her legs and Ari slipped between Rian's thighs as she moved her hand down and easily entered her wetness. Rian moved slightly opening herself allowing Ari to go deeper with each slow thrust.

She ran her hand down Ari's side as Ari lifted slightly encouraging her to go further. Reaching Ari's wet center, Rian moved her fingers around her clit in slow circles. Ari moaned deeply as Rian slipped two fingers inside her. Rian lifted her head and pressed her mouth to Ari's. They kissed passionately as they matched each other thrust for thrust. Ari rocked against her hand harder and harder as the pressure inside her built up. Rian was so close she could barely hold back any longer. Her body was begging for release.

Ari tightened around Rian's fingers and let out a guttural sound from deep inside. Rian watched the changes in her face as her body let go and then closed her eyes. She gave in to the pleasure she was seeking as she came so hard she saw dark spots when her eyes opened. She was gasping as she struggled to catch her breath. Ari kissed her softly and laid her head on Rian's chest. Her long blond hair cascaded across Rian's chest and shoulder. Rian ran her hands through the silky waves.

"I love you so damn much," Ari said when she raised her head and looked into Rian's eyes. Rian smiled and wrapped her arms tightly around her.

"I love you too. Something died inside of me when I thought I'd lost you, Ari," a tear escaped her watery eyes and Ari kissed it away.

"You'll never lose me again. I promise you, Rian. I want to spend the rest of my life with you. Damn the rest of the world."

~

The next day Rian ventured out to pick up the pictures from the Post Office box and arrange for a rental car. When she got back to the hotel, Ari was sitting on the bed casually in her robe drinking a cup of coffee.

Rian shook her head. "You're dangerous like that."

Ari smiled brightly. "Is that why you're standing so far away?"

"Yes," Rian stated frankly as she walked over the small table by the window. She sat in one of the two chairs and tossed the small package she retrieved on the table. Ari nonchalantly walked over to her and straddled her lap not caring that she was wet and it was soaking through Rian's pants.

"What about like this?" she said seductively as she rocked against her and ran her tongue around Rian's lips.

Rian slipped her hand under Ari and entered her slick center. Ari set the pace as she rode her slowly while matching her movements with a soft sensual kiss. Rian ran her other hand inside the robe and pushed it off her shoulders. It fell to floor between her feet. She moved her hand back across her chest rubbing each breast and squeezing each nipple back and forth. She caressed Ari's side and slowly moved her hand to caress her back and ass. She was careful not to break the contact as Ari continued riding her and kissing her slowly moving her tongue in and out of her mouth with each soft thrust of her hips.

Rian felt like she was dreaming as Ari swayed unhurriedly like she was dancing a slow waltz in her lap. Rian felt Ari tighten as she gasped against her mouth. She continued riding her slowly as she came. Rian's palm filled with her wetness. Ari relaxed as Rian withdrew her fingers and ran her palm up Ari's stomach to her chest spreading the warm wetness all over her. Ari rolled her bottom lip between her teeth.

Rian slipped her hands under Ari's ass and carried her to the bed. Ari sat up and removed Rian's shirt and bra as she pushed her wet pants and underwear to the floor. Rian moved on top of her and kissed her tenderly. Ari pushed Rian to the side and rolled on top of her. She broke the kiss as she slid down her body licking her breasts and nipples languorously. She finally reach Rian's center, hovered, and spread Rian's legs. When Rian's hips rose to meet her Ari moved lower as she ran her tongue down each leg to her ankle and back up to the crease of her thigh tantalizingly slow.

Rian moaned when Ari spread her lips and ran her tongue softly around her clit deliberately avoiding the pulsing center. Rian's toes curled and she bit her bottom lip hard. She was not sure if she could withstand the pressure building inside of her as Ari took her time gradually licking in circles. She began breathing heavily as Ari wrapped her lips around Rian's clit and sucked it into her mouth. Rian groaned loudly and lifted her hips to match each slow movement of Ari's mouth on her as Ari alternated licking and sucking at a very leisurely pace.

Rian had never made love so slowly in her life. She felt like her body was going to explode, her blood was boiling. She gripped the sheets with one hand and ran the other through Ari's hair. She felt the pressure rise to the surface burst into tiny electrical shocks as Ari slipped her tongue inside of her. She rode the climax as long as she could dragging out the last little bit at the end before her body went limp.

Ari ran her tongue back up Rian's body as she slid against her. Rian tasted herself on Ari's mouth and tongue as Ari kissed her. She wrapped her arms around her and held Ari tightly to her chest. She had no idea why or how the fates had changed in her favor bringing this incredible woman back into her life, but she thanked God everyday and promised to never take a second with her for granted.

"You amaze me," Rian said when Ari looked at her.

Ari smiled. "Is that so? You have no idea what you do to me." She kissed her again. "Still think I'm dangerous?"

"Hell yeah. You're down right devilish." Rian grinned and pushed Ari to the side and stood up. "But I love it," she said with a smile as she walked towards the bathroom.

~

Rian was looking at the pictures when Ari emerged from the bathroom freshly showered and dressed in jeans and a thin sweater. She joined her at the table and picked up the first photo she saw.

"This is Val," she said as she set it back down.

"I figured as much. There are a bunch of pictures here with him and Walsh together," Rian said as she put the photos in the lock box with the rest of the Intel she had on Canturri and put the box back inside the backpack.

"What do we do now?"

"Pack and get some sleep. We're crossing the border in the morning," Rian said.

"I don't have any identification. That's going to be a problem."

"Not anymore," Rian said as she handed her a Canadian I.D. with a picture of a woman that looked close enough to be her twin.

Ari examined it and nodded. "Do I want to know how and where you got this?"

"Nope," Rian said.

Ari laughed.

Rian didn't want to explain how she followed a woman that resembled Ari all over the shopping strip that morning causing her to waste two hours of her time until the woman went to finally pay for something. The female cashier asked for her I.D. and Rian ran to the counter yelling that someone was on the floor bleeding and needed help. Both women ran to the area to help the person and Rian swiped the I.D. from the counter and exited through the fire door.

Chapter Twenty

Rian was driving the small rental car when they approached the car check line for the Canada/United States border. She rolled down the window when it was their turn. She and Ari were both wearing sunglasses and she hoped they didn't ask Ari to remove hers. Their suitcase was stored in the trunk.

"Good morning, ladies," The man in uniform took the I.D.'s Rian handed him. "I'll need your car registration also."

Rian handed him the rental agreement.

"What's your purpose for crossing the border today?" he asked.

"We're going to spend the day at the casino and see Niagra Falls from the American side. She's never been to the United States." Rian said with as much of a French accent as she could muster and nodded at Ari.

"Our sides better," the man said.

"I tried to tell her that," she smiled.

The man looked at the papers and their I.D.'s again. "You plan on returning today, correct?"

"Yes sir," Rian said. "I can't afford fancy American hotels."

The man laughed and handed their information back to Rian. "Enjoy your trip," he said as he pushed the button. The barricade bar rose slowly and Rian drove under it. She heard Ari let out a heavy breath that she'd obviously been holding.

"I was hoping he didn't ask me anything," Ari said.

"Me too. We would've been toast. You're sweet and innocent voice could never sound French," Rian laughed. "You can relax now. We have a ten hour drive."

"Are we going straight to D.C.?"

"Yes. Well close enough anyway. If Walsh thinks we're dead, he won't be looking for us. He won't have any of his cronies looking for us either. Remember we're traveling as Canadians."

Rian stopped at the first casino she saw and rushed inside to exchange the couple of hundred Canadian Dollars she was carrying into U.S. Dollars.

"Did you put it all on thirteen and let it ride?" Ari smiled.

"Thought about it," Rian said as she started the car and got back on the highway.

~

They crossed into Maryland eight hours later. Ari was sleeping in the passenger seat next to Rian. She smiled and pulled over to use the payphone at a gas station and grab a cup of coffee. She dialed the number she had written down on a piece of paper in her pocket.

"It's me. We're back in the States," Rian said.

"Is it safe?" Leann said.

"Safe enough. Everyone thinks we're dead."

"That guy Walsh questioned me a few days ago. He was asking how well I knew you and if you may have left anything in my possession. He also wanted to know if I knew why you were flying towards Canada and if I knew who you were traveling with."

"What did you say to him?"

"I made you out to be the asshole you were when you first got here. I told him I knew you and worked with you occasionally, but I didn't know you well enough to know anything about your personal life. I think he was pretty much convinced after he talked to Carl Quinn. I'm sure he gave you a raving review," she laughed.

Rian laughed too. "That's good to know."

"By the way, Steven Monahan was arraigned on multiple murders charges the other day. Apparently, Quinn found a map in the guy's basement that had the location of each of his victims marked. He also had a notepad with pages and pages of notes that pertained to J.P. so I can safely assume you were probably right the entire time. Too bad you're supposedly dead. Quinn's going to get all the credit for solving this case."

"He's a piece of shit. Captain Burke needs to give you the majority of the credit. Hell, if it wasn't for you pushing me we probably would've never come up with the information we did."

"Yeah, I know, but I'm only a medical examiner to them unfortunately the good ol' boy network still exists."

"No kidding."

"How is everything going?" Leann asked.

"So far so good. I need to figure out how to get a passport for Ari and fast. I have a feeling Walsh is going to take a trip real soon. I got her an I.D. in Toronto with a close enough picture to get her across the border."

Leann laughed. "Do I even want to know?"

"Nope."

"Give me a day or two. I may have something for you," Leann said.

"Sounds good. I need to go. Dump this phone you're on. I'll send you another one in the morning."

Rian got back in the car with two cups of coffee as Ari was waking up. She handed her a cup.

"Where are we?"

"Maryland. We should be at the hotel in about two hours." Rian said.

~

They arrived at the hotel and Rian checked them in. Ari went up to the room while Rian took a drive into Washington, D.C. and swapped out the rental car for a new one. She didn't recognize anyone she saw on the streets as she cruised around. She drove by the FBI building and parked down the street a little ways to wait as the sun began to set. She watched every car coming out of the parking garage until she saw the unmarked car pass in front of her with Walsh alone in the driver's seat. She wrote down the tag number and pulled out into traffic a few cars behind him.

Rian watched as Walsh pulled into the driveway of a brownstone close to DuPont Circle. She was surprised to see that they lived that close to each other. The apartment she and Ari shared was less than a mile away. She wrote down the address and waited long enough to make sure that was his actual address and not just a stop he was making on his way home.

Rian arrived back at the hotel a few hours later. Ari was sitting by the window watching the cars pass on the street below.

"Where did you go?" she asked when Rian closed the door.

"D.C."

Ari raised an eyebrow. "Did you see anyone you know?"

"Walsh," Rian said as she sat down and took her shoes off. "I needed to see where he lived."

"What the hell for? Did he see you?"

"No. Don't forget, I have the same training he does, if not more. I worked at lot of areas he didn't, but he spent a lot of time with his nose up someone's ass and taking advancement tests instead of actually investigating anything. That's why he was promoted, but that was years ago. Anyway, I need to plan our next move and I can only do that if I know his next move. It's like chess."

Ari rolled her eyes. "That figures. You know I hate that game. Please be careful. I don't like being this close to him or any of them for that matter."

"Me either. Hopefully, this will all be over soon," Rian said as she kissed her briefly before going to take a shower.

~

The next morning Rian was sitting in her rental car a few houses down from Walsh's brownstone. The sun was just starting to come over the horizon when the front door opened and Walsh made his way to the black unmarked car in the driveway. Rian ducked down low enough to still see him, but remain out of his sightline. The car backed out of the driveway and she pulled away from the curb a few car lengths behind. She followed him all the way to the FBI building. Once she was sure he was inside she circled back around and parked along the curb a couple of houses down from Walsh's.

Satisfied no one was around, she quickly walked up to the back door of the brownstone and pulled her lock picking kit from her pocket. She hoped there wasn't an alarm, but she hadn't seen the box anywhere when she walked around the house, so she figured Walsh wasn't paranoid enough for security protection. She knew he was divorced, so more than likely no one else lived with him and he wasn't animal friendly so there wouldn't be a vicious dog waiting for her.

Rian entered the house and closed the door. She waited and listened for the alarm beeping, but there was only silence and the occasional creaking of an old house. She walked through the kitchen and dining room to the living room before taking the stairs to the second floor. The door was open to one of the rooms at the end of the hall. She assumed that was Walsh's bedroom when she saw the unmade bed. She decided to go in the only other room up there. She opened the door and smiled when she saw the large desk and file cabinet. She hoped Walsh was as careless as she thought he was. Anyone with enough stupidity to get involved with a mob crime boss wasn't exactly the sharpest crayon in the box to start with. She still couldn't believe he would throw his life away like that. Whatever he thought he was getting out of the deal was surely a lie. Fiorino Canturri didn't *deal* with people. The more she thought about it the more it pissed her off to know this was going on behind her back during the time she was the lead agent on the case. No wonder her Intel was always all over the board, nothing in the case was ever consistent. More than likely it was because Walsh was sabotaging the case the entire time.

Rian went through the desk drawers one at a time. The only thing she found was paid bills and tax information. The filing cabinet was locked which meant it probably held incriminating evidence and without a way to make copies she wouldn't be able to take anything anyway, so she went back to the desk and began shuffling through the stack of unpaid bills. In the middle of the pile, she found a notepad with an airline name, flight number, and time printed in his sloppy handwriting. She wrote everything on the notepad from her pocket and put the pile back the way she found it. She looked at the filing cabinet one more time. She'd already been in there too long so she walked out of the room and hurried down the stairs.

When she exited the house she watched the nearby houses for any sign of people, apparently everyone worked in the neighborhood because it was quiet and empty. She walked briskly to her car and drove off.

~

"Do I even want to know how and where you got this?" Ari asked with a grin as she read the notepad.

Rian smiled. "Probably not," she said as she dialed a number on her cell phone and waited.

"Hello?" Leann whispered.

"Can you talk?"

"Hold on," she said as she walked out of the building. "I was walking out of Captain Burke's office."

"Is everything okay?" Rian asked.

"Yes, I was just giving him a report he asked for."

"Are you any closer on the passport for Ari?"

"It's almost done. I needed a picture or her, but I googled her and sure enough a picture popped up. She has beautiful eyes."

"Yes she does," Rian looked over at Ari and smiled.

"Thanks to Photoshop she now has brown hair and brown eyes. Hopefully, she won't be recognized. Her name is Kristen Olsen."

"Great. Where did you find that?"

"An unclaimed from last month had a passport on her. I swiped it and rewrote the property log. I made a few changes to fit Ari's description and swapped the photos."

"Be careful, Leann. You never know if you're being watched."

"I keep looking for a tail, but so far nothing. I always talk to you outside of the building and there is nothing in my apartment but pictures and personal stuff. As far as they know I don't know you very well and you're dead."

"I hope it stays that way. Anyway, when will the passport be ready?"

"I'll have it in the mail today."

"Good. I also need you to look up a flight for me," Rian said. She read her all of the information she copied from Walsh's notepad. "You should probably go to the library to use the computer so you can cover your tracks."

"Okay. I'll go on my lunch break and overnight the passport and then stop by the library. I'll call you when I know something," Leann said.

Rian hung up and walked over to Ari. "Your passport will be here tomorrow. We need to dye your hair brown again. Do you still have those brown contacts?"

"Yes. When are we leaving?"

"I don't know. Leann's going to get back to me this afternoon with the flight information. My guess is probably sooner than later."

"I should probably color it tonight then," Ari said.

"Leann thinks you have beautiful eyes by the way," Rian grinned. "I definitely agree with her, but I am a little biased since I'm head over heels in love with you."

"You better watch out 007, you might have some competition," Ari joked.

"Uh huh," Rian pulled Ari against her and kissed her tenderly.

~

Rian watched Ari dye her beautiful natural blond hair to plain brown, thankfully the dye was temporary. It was still odd seeing her like that. She was so use to having her Ari back. This dark hair and dark eyed person felt like a stranger. She jumped as the cell phone on the table rang. She answered it quickly.

"The information you gave me is for a flight from Washington, D.C. to Buenos Aires, Argentina leaving this Friday at six in the evening and arriving Saturday around one in the afternoon," Leann said.

"Thanks."

"Who's on that flight?"

"Walsh."

"How did you find that out?" Leann asked.

"The old fashioned way," Rian said. "I need you to do one more thing. Go to a different library and book a one-way flight from Baltimore to Rosario, Province of Santa Fe, Argentina to arrive Friday. Two first class passengers, Kristen Olsen and Olivia Dawson," Rian said. She also gave her the number for the credit card she'd been using. "Also, book us a small SUV to be picked up at the airport and returned at the airport next Monday. Book it in Olivia

Dawson's name. That's the name on the credit card I just gave you."

"Are you sure about this?" Leann asked.

"More than sure. It's time for this shit to end, one way or another," Rian said.

"Please be careful," Leann paused. "Both of you."

"Call me with our flight and rental car information as soon as you have it, then dump that phone."

"How will I know if you're okay?"

"When it's over I'll get word to you, I promise," Rian said.

Chapter Twenty-One

Rian and Ari landed in Argentina after a long eighteen hour flight. They went through customs easily and grabbed their rented shoebox sized SUV. A quick trip around the large city led them back to a five star hotel close to the airport and a huge shopping district. They ate an early dinner and stopped at a few of the shops to prepare for the three hour drive to Buenos Aires. Ari had been fairly quiet since their arrival to her home country. Rian hoped it wasn't a mistake bringing her along. She wondered if her plans were going to be too much for Ari to handle. She watched her sleep as she drove through the country towards Ari's own personal hell.

Rian reached Buenos Aires and took the back roads to the farmlands on the other side of the city to a remote area just outside of the city limits near the coast that she remembered from her previous trip. After arriving at her destination she parked and turned the car off. Ari gently stirred, then opened her eyes. The sun had just set and there were no city lights to illuminate their surroundings and she struggled to see in the pitch black. Rian was looking out the windshield through a pair of secondhand night vision goggles that she'd picked up in the used surplus store near the military base a half hour away.

"What do you have?" Ari said.

"Binoculars. I stopped at the store while you were sleeping," Rian answered. She was watching for any signs of life on the other side of the woods.

"Where are we?" Ari asked. Rian handed her the night vision goggles and adjusted them for her. Ari looked at the structure lit up with green light in the lenses. She quickly pushed the goggles off her head. "Rian!" she yelled. "Are you crazy? That's my father's compound."

"I know that," Rian said as she took the goggles and put them back on.

"What if they see us?"

"They won't. It's quiet. I haven't seen anyone, not even the guard."

"What are we doing here?"

"I'm looking for a way in. Walsh's plane arrives early in the morning. I can safely assume he will come straight here. I have a very small window."

"You're going in there? You've definitely lost your mind. They will kill you, Rian."

"They won't even know I'm there. You have to trust me, Ari."

"What are you going to do if your plan works and you get in?"

Rian took the goggles off and looked at Ari. "What do you know about your mother?"

"What do you mean?"

"What happened to your mother? Where is she? What did your father tell you?"

"Why are you asking me this, Rian?"

"Just answer me, Ari. Please?"

"I don't know," she paused to think about it. "I was pretty little when my father told me about her. He said she ran off to another country when I was a baby, she just left us."

Rian looked back through the windshield into the darkness. "During my time investigating your father I ran across a piece of information that didn't quite fit in the puzzle so I came down here to research it. This was probably just before you left home. I never came anywhere near his compound. I was only here to search the city records," she hesitated. "I put the new information that I found together with my Intel when I got back home. Do you know your mother's name? Or how she knew your father? Did he tell you any of that?"

"No. Well, once he did call her Marcella, which I assumed was her name. That topic was not discussed in the house. He told me she left us and that was the end of it. What do you know, Rian?"

"She didn't leave you, Ari. She was a maid for your father's compound that he used in any way he felt like using her and she got pregnant with you. When you were only a couple of months old she tried to flee the country with you."

"How do you know this? What happened to her?"

"He killed her, Ari. I'm sorry," Rian pulled Ari against her and wiped the tears from her face. "We had most of the names of the present and past employees of Fiorino Canturri over the years and we traced each one as far as we could. Some of them actually spoke and gave us valuable information. When I found a gardener that retired from working at the compound, I tracked him all the way to France. He was the one that told me the story of your mother. He said she was young under twenty he thought with blond hair and blue eyes. She was from Uruguay. He said she tried to leave because she didn't want you growing up with that monster."

"What did he do to her?" Ari sniffed and tried to dry the tears that kept falling.

"Are you sure you want to know all of this?"

"Yes. Please tell me."

"Do you know your Uncle Diego very well?" Rian asked.

"He's my father's brother, his right-hand man. Of course, I know him. He lives on the compound."

"Fiorino decided to test Diego's loyalty with orders to put your mother in the ocean with cement boots. When Diego finished the job Fiorino knew he could be trusted so he promoted him to the position he still holds today."

"Oh my god, Rian."

"I'm really sorry," Rian held her across the console and kissed the top of her head. "He must have a thing for water because the son of bitch put me in the middle of the damn ocean too, only he left me alive thinking I would die a slow agonizing death after his men beat the shit out of me."

"I know," Ari said.

Rian pulled back and looked at her. "What?"

"I was there. I knew what was going on and there was nothing I could do to stop him. That's why I took off to the States to see if you survived. I had to know. When I saw you I was so relieved and so scared he would find out."

"That's when you sent the letters?"

"Yes. I couldn't let him hurt you anymore. I guess Walsh had someone watching you because as soon as he found out I was near you he told my father. I caught on very quickly when I spotted Val in Portland. I'm sure he was sent there to kill us both. Val is in line to take over one day and he thinks our father is some kind of god or something, he'd do anything for him. Including killing his own sister."

"Why didn't you tell me?"

"That's when I made the decision to reveal myself to you. I couldn't let him take you from me, not again."

"Was he on the plane to D.C.?"

"Yes. I don't think he knew the FBI agent that was following you though. My father works alone. I doubt he involved Walsh. He's more like a puppet for my father than the business partner he thinks he is. My father has no business partners. Everyone works *for* him, not *with* him. We must have lost Val in the airport when we ditched the FBI agent. I never saw him again."

"I can't believe you're just now telling me this, Ari. Damn it we were in a far worse situation than I thought," Rian shook her head.

"I thought if I told you about Val you might think I was working with him. You were barely speaking to me, Rian. You thought I betrayed you. I was so scared of losing you again, I couldn't say anything. Then, he disappeared so there was no reason to tell you."

"Don't ever keep anything from me ever again, Ari. Your secrets are going to be the damn death of me. Is there anything else you're not telling me?"

"No. I'm sorry, Rian. I didn't do any of it to hurt you. I was trying to protect you from my family."

"I don't need protecting. You should know that by now."

"I can definitely see that. I never knew this side of you, Rian. It intrigues me and scares me a little. You went to work and came home every day without talking about your job. You never brought work home. I had no idea what being an FBI agent really entailed. I was naive and so in love with you. I didn't care about anything else, not even the fact that you were an FBI agent and I was Fiorino Canturri's daughter. I didn't care. I don't care."

"Do you care about your father? Or any of your family for that matter?"

"No. Not anymore," Ari sighed. "They have taken so much from me. Hate isn't even a strong enough for word for what I feel for them. All of them."

Rian kissed her softly and ran the back of her hand over Ari's cheek. "We better get going, we've been here longer than I wanted and I have another stop to make."

"What are you going to do to them?"

181

"What do you want me to do?" Rian said as she started the car and looked at Ari in the faint moonlight.

"Kill them. Kill them all," Ari said.

Chapter Twenty-Two

At midnight Rian parked the car a few miles from her destination and told Ari to take off in the opposite direction if she spotted anyone but Rian coming her way. Rian kissed her and took off in the darkness. She was dressed all in black with black face paint covering her entire face. She ran the short distance and crossed the wide ditch careful not to step in the muddy water. On the other side, she found the chain link fence and pulled a pair of wire cutters from her pocket. She quickly clipped enough links to peel the fence up enough to slip through the bottom. The fence moved back into place as she moved away from it.

The Army base was small and most of the buildings were old and dilapidated. She took her penlight out of her pocket and put the cutters back. She maneuvered in the dark staying away from the spotlights, crawling under vehicles at a few points. She checked each building until she found the one marked *Municiones*, Munitions. She pulled the lock pick set from her other pocket and began working the locks. Seconds passed before she pulled the squeaky metal door open, slipped through, and closed it quickly behind her. She waited a minute to see if anyone heard the door before turning on her penlight and searching through each room in the small building. She collected bits and pieces of military armaments until the black backpack she was wearing was full. She zipped it closed and moved back towards the door.

She cracked the door open and she noticed the guard walking near the building across from her. She held her breath and kept the door cracked just enough to see him. He disappeared around the corner and she swung the door open and slammed it closed. She dove for cover behind a truck parked nearby and watched as the guard came running across the asphalt towards the Munitions building. She backed away from the truck and circled around. She grabbed a small rock and hurled it in the opposite direction. It made a loud thud as it bounced off the metal building across from her. The guard drew his gun and turned around to run in the direction of the sound. Rian waited until he was gone. Quietly she followed the fence line running behind the buildings, careful to hide anytime she heard footsteps.

When she reached the opening in the fence she pulled it back and pushed the backpack through, slid under, and pulled the fence back into place. She ran to the ditch, ducked down inside the drainpipe, and waited. She couldn't believe how easy it was to infiltrate the base. Their security was obviously severely lacking. After a few minutes she popped her head up and was surprised to see nothing had changed. Apparently the guard never went back to check the door. She shook her head and took off running towards the car parked a mile away.

Reaching the car, she placed the backpack on the back floorboard, slipped into the driver's seat and started the car.

"Where have you been?" Ari asked

"Ari, have you ever heard of don't ask, don't tell?"

Ari shrugged. "Yes."

"Good, you don't ask and I won't have to tell you," Rian said as she put the car in gear and sped off in the opposite direction.

~

They drove in silence towards the farmlands a half hour away. Rian parked the car in the same spot she had been in only hours before overlooking the compound. She turned the car off and left the keys in the ignition as she turned towards Ari.

"I want you to get in the driver's seat, lock the doors, keep the windows up, and wait for me. I'm going to be gone for a little while. If I haven't returned in two hours, or you see anyone coming towards you start the car and drive off as fast as you can."

"I'm not leaving you there, Rian. No."

"Damn it, Ari. Just do it."

"Promise me you'll come back," she said.

"I promise. I love you, Ari." Rian kissed her soft lips and got out of the car. She grabbed the backpack from the back seat, added a couple of remaining items, and a few more tools.

"There's a gate on the South corner that leads from the gardens to a secret exit from the compound. That's how I always snuck out. Just follow the wall until you come to a thin metal panel. That's the gate. Pull it towards you to open it. You'll be in the middle of the gardens a few hundred yards from the main house," Ari rolled the window back up and watched her as far as she could in the darkness. Rian quickly disappeared in the middle of the woods.

~

Rian followed the path towards the south corner of the compound. She stayed in the shadow of the fence out of the moonlight. It took her close to twenty minutes to reach the gate. It was after three a.m. and she was sure most of the house was asleep. She pulled the gate open and stepped inside. She had an eerie feeling that caused her skin to crawl. She took a deep breath and pulled the gate shut. The only guard on duty was at the main gate. She hadn't seen anyone walking the perimeter when she sat in the car watching the compound. She bent down and pulled the night vision goggles from the backpack. The entire compound lit up in a green glowing light in front of her.

She ran towards the main house and hid next to the pool house. She pulled a spool of thin wire from the bag and a brick of C4 explosive putty. She rolled the putty into multiple thin strips and began placing it in the window seals and door jams close by. She pulled a blasting cap from the bag and cut the wire into two small strips. She attached the two wires to the blasting cap and pulled one of the throw away cell phones from the bag that she'd picked up at a small store on their way back to the hotel. She took the back cover off and attached the opposite end of the wire to the battery leads.

She buried the phone in the dirt next to the bushes and continued around to the next side of the house where she started the process all over again. Once she had all four sides of the house rigged she took the rest of the putty and rolled it into clumps and tossed it up on the low hanging areas of each roof of the two smaller buildings. Rian went to the three cars parked in the circular driveway and put rolls of putty up under each car inside the frame and rigged a blasting cap and cell phone to the car in the middle. The entire procedure took over an hour. She checked her watch. She had less than twenty minutes to get back to Ari before she drove off without her and she was over a mile away.

Rian closed up the backpack and ran as fast as she could through the garden towards the gate in the corner. She moved through it quickly and took off running again towards the car on the other side of the thick woods. She tripped over a root and flew through the air landing on her knee and held in the loud scream she wanted to let out. Her knee was in excruciating pain as she started running again at a slightly slower pace. She checked her watch again. Her two hour window had come and gone. She finally reached the edge of the woods close to fifteen minutes late. She shook her head and said a prayer when she saw the car a few feet away. She limped towards it as Ari jumped out and rushed to her.

"What happened? Are you okay?"

"I'm fine. I fell and smashed up my knee," Rian hugged her tightly, then drew away and got in the driver's side of the car. Ari walked around to the passenger side and got in.

"What do we do now?" Ari said.

"We wait," Rian said. She kept her goggles on the compound until the sun came up. She switched to regular binoculars and watched as the compound came alive. She saw multiple guys outside walking around smoking cigarettes. When a small car approached the gate she sat up straight.

Ari was dozing in the seat next to her. She leaned over and bumped her. "Wake up, baby."

"What's going on?" Ari said as she yawned and stretched.

"I think Walsh just arrived."

She watched the car come to a stop and the guard at the gate got in the passenger side.

The car proceeded up the driveway and parked behind the other cars. When the driver stepped out Rian was sure it was Walsh, there was no mistaking his shape.

"This is it," she said.

Ari strained her eyes to see, but she could only see the outline of the compound.

"Do you like fireworks, Ari?" Rian asked as she watched the men enter the house.

"Yes, who doesn't?"

188

"Good." Rian put down the binoculars and picked up her cell phone. Each of the phones she wired up as detonators were programmed into her phone and set up for two three-way calls. She checked her watch and waited five more minutes. Then, she dialed the first three-way call. The first three phones buried in the dirt began to vibrate and the shock had enough power going to the wires to set off the blasting caps. Each one ignited in a small explosion that set the C4 off.

All of a sudden there were multiple explosions that rocked the ground hard enough to shake the car they were sitting in a mile away. Rian quickly dialed the other call and the cars exploded in balls of fire that pushed them up off the ground. The house and two buildings next to the cars blew to pieces with flames licking the sky and fragments floating to the ground. The entire compound looked like a war zone as black smoke filled the air.

Rian knew what justice was and what it felt like, and she'd heard of bittersweet revenge, but she didn't know what that felt like until now.

"Oh my god," Ari whispered as she watched in shock. She was surprised that she didn't shed a single tear for the monster she called Father as she watched the inferno.

Rian kept the binoculars trained on the area and was satisfied when she saw no one escaped the horrendous blast. They stayed parked there long enough to watch the remains burn to the ground. The authorities and fire trucks were beginning to head in that direction as they drove away.

They crossed a bridge over the river and Rian tossed her cell phone out the window over the top of the car. It flew over the side of the bridge and sank to the bottom before their car was even off the bridge.

"How did you know how to do all of that?" Ari asked softly.

Rian looked over at her and grabbed her hand. "You'd be surprised at what the American Government taught me," she said as she looked back at the road.

Ari turned her head towards the window. She wasn't sure if she believed her, but she had no other choice. There was no reason to pry into Rian's past. She knew better than anyone about having a past you wanted to forget. Thanks to Rian, a murdering monster was no longer a threat to the world and their lives were no longer in jeopardy.

"Where are we going?"

"The airport," Rian smiled. "You have a few hours to decide our next destination."

Epilogue

Rian was sitting on the balcony of their rented apartment reading the news on her laptop and watching the gondolas in the water down below. She and Ari had been in Venice close to six months with no sign of trouble from the U.S. or Argentina. Rian scanned pages and pages of national news and Buenos Aires news daily looking for any indication that the authorities had a lead. After the first couple of days, the explosion slowly became old news.

When Rian finally got word to Leann she was surprised to hear the news of the blast in Argentina had become national news. Leann asked her if she had anything to do with it and Rian simply reminded her of don't ask, don't tell. The less she knew the better off she was.

Ari walked outside and sat down in the chair next to Rian. The diamond on her left hand glistened in the sunlight. Rian was shocked when Ari pulled the ring from her pocket the day they arrived in Venice and asked her to put it back on her hand.

"Anything good in the news?" Ari asked.

Rian took a sip of her coffee. "So far nothing interesting," she said as she continued to read. She gasped and turned pale. Ari watched the mug she was holding hit the concrete and smash into pieces as hot coffee splashed the ground. Rian turned the computer towards Ari.

The bold headline read: *Explosion Survivor Leaves Hospital.*

"Oh my god," Ari whispered.

About the Author

Graysen Morgen was born and raised in North Florida with winding rivers and waterways at her back door and the white sandy beach a mile away. She has spent most of her lifetime in the sun and on the water. She enjoys reading, writing, fishing, and spending as much time as possible with her partner and their daughter.

You can contact Graysen at graysenmorgen@aol.com and like her fan page on facebook.com/graysenmorgen

www.ingramcontent.com/pod-product-compliance
Lightning Source LLC
Chambersburg PA
CBHW072111170626
46813CB00004B/1507